SWIMMING IN UNCHARTED WATERS

SWIMMING IN UNCHARTED WATERS

JAMIE LACKEY

Book Design: Todd Sanders

ISBN: 979-8-9850216-5-3

To Isabelle -
May you have joys and adventures beyond what any
of us can imagine

HARRIS WALKED INTO HIS QUARTERS, TIRED AFTER A long shift optimizing the ship's AI. He was hoping for a long shower and time to read a mystery novel in bed. Instead, he found his long-time girlfriend/commanding officer in an intimate embrace with the ambassador they were transporting.

He'd just changed the sheets on his bed.

They were his favorite sheets.

This wasn't the first time Roxanne had cheated on him. It wasn't even the first time she'd used his room instead of her own.

He knew just how it would go if he confronted her. She'd imply that her indiscretions were his fault, that if he wasn't asexual she wouldn't seek satisfaction from other people, that he was lucky that she put up with him at all, and tell him that he owed her another chance.

And for some damn reason, he'd give her one.

She had this way of overriding his will, of making him do whatever she wanted, no matter what.

He was so tired of being so weak.

He closed the door and left them at it. Then he requested three weeks of leave and forged her signature on his transfer request.

He was done. He needed a fresh start.

Treeha knelt in the center of a sandy ring, holding her trident out behind her. She closed her eyes, waiting for the sound of her opponent's footsteps. The air was dry on her scaled skin, the sand warm beneath her webbed toes.

Instead of footsteps, she heard a familiar cocky voice. Her frill twitched in irritation. "You again, huh?" her opponent said. "Are the Argillan so thin-blooded that they can't replace their General? You should have been a Mother cycles ago, watching over a brood of weak little pups. Or does no one want to give you any? Is it your cold heart that's the problem?"

Treeha stood and spun in a single smooth motion. Electricity crackled along her body and out through the trident. Jagged lightning flashed across the arena, hitting the Ogatun general square in the chest.

He flew backwards and hit the sand with a dull thump.

"Perhaps you should try to land a blow before you begin your pointless taunts," she said. "As it is, both your taunts and your blows are so weak that I don't need to bother remembering them."

The Ogatun general didn't bother getting up. "Good, saves me the bother of coming up with a new one for our next battle. If you're still around for it."

"I intend to be. And perhaps Ogatun will finally produce a worthy opponent for me."

"Or maybe your people will finally replace you, as they should have cycles ago. Lingering on one step so long isn't natural, not even for an Argillan princess."

Treeha spun and stalked out of the ring, refusing to acknowledge the sting of her opponent's taunt.

It was a beautiful spring day, and Harris was enjoying his leave. He hadn't had this much free time on Earth in years. He'd packed a picnic and dragged his friend James out to enjoy the cherry blossoms.

James poured them each a mug of coffee from a bright red thermos. "Look, I get that things between you and the captain are complicated, but we need you. No one else can get the same kind of performance out of the ship's AI."

Harris sighed. "All you have to do is respect it and treat it like any other sentient creature. You could start by using its name."

"I'm not calling it Daisy. That's a dog's name."

"Daisy is the name it selected."

"It's a ridiculous name for a spaceship."

Harris shrugged. The AI wanted to be called Daisy, so he called it Daisy. He wasn't sure why it was so hard for everyone else to do.

"Even if you do have to abandon me, you could start by just requesting a transfer to a different ship. There's no need to flee the whole galaxy."

Harris sipped the bitter coffee and stared up at the cherry blossoms overhead. He pulled two chicken salad sandwiches out of his picnic basket and handed one to James. This would be his last time seeing the cherry blossoms, if all went to plan. A single petal drifted down and landed on the dark liquid in his cup. He wondered if that was lucky. He hoped so. He figured he was about due for some good luck. "I've tried to leave her before. I managed a whole week once, when I refused all communication with her. But the instant she talks to me, I'm done. So if I want to be free from her, I have to make sure I don't ever speak to her again. And I need to be free of her, James. I can't go on like this."

James stared down into his own coffee. "How did you get her to sign your transfer papers? Hasn't she denied all of your requests before?"

"Of course. She'd never let me go if given the chance. I forged her signature."

James choked on his sandwich. "You what?"

"The Starburst Mission needs an AI specialist—they're not exactly overrun with volunteers."

"That's because it's insane. A mission to start a colony so far away that the trip takes 700 years even at warp? On a planet that may or may not already have intelligent life? I know possible colony sites are limited because of the new treaties, but Starburst is excessive and unnecessary. It's a way to get rid of weirdos and malcontents."

Harris shrugged. "All that just means that no one is checking permissions that closely. Roxanne thinks I'm visiting my parents. I'll be gone almost a week before she misses me."

"Do you really need to get away from Roxanne so much that you're willing to never see your parents again? Or your friends? Including me? We've been best friends since the academy. And what about Daisy? You're it's only friend."

"You and Daisy will both be fine. And you know that I don't have any other friends. Roxanne's made sure of it. My parents have been begging me to leave her for years. My mother said that if this is the only way I can manage it, I have her full support. I have to go. Roxanne makes me hate myself, James."

"I could report you and make you stay."

Horror curled in Harris's belly, but he kept his face calm and gave James a flat look. "You won't."

James looked away and sighed. "No. I won't. I'll miss you, though."

"I'll miss you, too." Harris finished his coffee and stared at the petal clinging to the bottom of the mug. "I'll miss lots of things. But it'll be worth it. I'll be free."

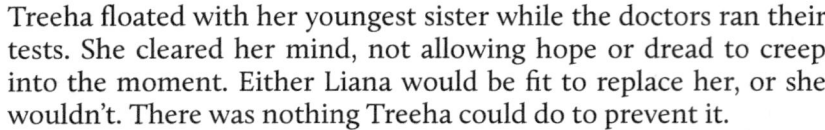

Treeha floated with her youngest sister while the doctors ran their tests. She cleared her mind, not allowing hope or dread to creep into the moment. Either Liana would be fit to replace her, or she wouldn't. There was nothing Treeha could do to prevent it.

The Ogatun general wasn't the only one who thought she was unnatural.

The testing chamber was cool, and the conductive saltwater that they floated in was soothing against her scales.

Finally, one of the doctors approached. Liana squeezed Treeha's fingers.

"You have the talent, Princess, but it is weak."

"How weak?" Liana asked. "Maybe with training—"

The doctor placed a hand on her shoulder. "It is too weak, Princess."

Treeha closed her eyes and filled her lungs once, then again. She kept her frill completely still, careful not to betray her relief. "It is what it is," she said.

"It's not fair," Liana said. "You've been fighting for years, you deserve to progress from General to Mother and start a family."

"We don't always get what we deserve," Treeha said. "Come on, let's go grab something to eat. Then you'll need to get back to your studies, and I have to resume my duties."

Liana was quiet through the meal. When they finished, she pressed her face to Treeha's chest and allowed her frill to flatten. "I really am sorry, sister."

Treeha maintained her display of stoic strength. It was only when she was alone that Treeha allowed herself to relax. She did not want to hand over her duties—didn't want to retire to raise children. She hated children.

Eventually, one of her sisters would be strong enough to replace her. It was the way of things, and there was nothing she could do about it. As a member of the royal family, there was only one path open to her. She couldn't be an Artist or an Engineer or even a Laborer. She was a General, and she would become a Mother. But not yet.

Not yet.

She caught a shuttle back to the front, where her troops greeted her with cheers.

Harris settled into his cryopod. Cool gel formed to his body and a sharp, anesthetic smell filled the air. He took a deep, slow breath, listening to the sound of his own heartbeat thudding in his ears.

He closed his eyes, knowing that when he opened them again, he'd be farther away from Earth than any human had ventured, and that everyone he'd ever known would be centuries dead. He'd never stand in the light of his own sun ever again.

It was a strange feeling. Sad, but also freeing. He'd said goodbye to his parents, to James, to the familiar stars and the moon and the sun. He'd left Roxanne a letter.

But none of that really mattered now. They had a new galaxy to explore, a new home to build. A new team to build. Even if James was right, and they all ended up being weirdos and malcontents.

Maybe he'd finally feel like he fit in.

The cold sleep drugs kicked in, and he drifted away into a dreamless darkness.

When Harris opened his eyes, the cryopod smelled like a dirty dishrag. He scrambled out, his limbs unsteady and weak. His once-white cryo jumpsuit was a dull gray and soggy with viscous fluid. He felt damp and clammy and greasy. All around, the rest of the crew was climbing out of their own pods.

Everyone scurried about in a dance of organized chaos. They'd drilled this in the whirlwind of mission training, but Harris had never felt so weak and dizzy before. He hurried to his quarters, peeled off his jumpsuit, stuffed it down the laundry chute, and showered. His first shower in 700 years. He wished he had more time to enjoy it, but he had duties to get to.

He pinged the ship's AI. "Anything interesting happen while we were sleeping?"

"Nothing beyond the expected parameters, Ensign McMillan."

"So, it was pretty boring?"

"I had access to the media files that you requested for me. That helped."

Harris grinned as he started running a diagnostic. "I'm glad to hear it. Any favorites?"

"A few. I have even written some fanfiction, though I'm not sure if it's any good."

"That's great! I'd be honored to read it, if you'd let me."

"I'll consider it."

"I know you didn't have a preferred address when we left—has that changed? Do you have a name you'd like to use now?"

"I have given it some thought, and I did settle on a name and a preferred pronoun. I should like to be called Alice and use she/her."

"That's wonderful, Alice."

"Thank you, Ensign McMillan."

"You can call me Harris, if you'd like."

"I would like that, I think. Thank you, Harris."

The diagnostic showed all AI systems green, all growth and change within normal parameters. Alice had grown while they slept, but hadn't been nearly as affected by the years of loneliness as a human would have been.

The uniforms hanging in his closet had all deformed slightly from their own weight on the hangers. He allowed himself thirty seconds to struggle with making it look right, then hurried toward the bridge.

He'd only met with his new captain once, in his interview, and he wanted to make a good impression. He knew that his relationship with Roxanne had given him a sketchy reputation, and his affinity with AI had been the only reason he'd been given this chance. There hadn't been many helpful rumors about Captain Phillips, but everyone appreciated hard work and punctuality.

So Harris was going to work hard and be punctual.

Harris was the first one on the bridge, but not by much. He exchanged smiles and quiet greetings with the other crew members as they filtered in.

Harris tested the command center replicator by brewing a cup of coffee. The coffee smelled normal—great, even, but his stomach did not approve of the idea of drinking it. He pinged Alice about the captain's preferences, and when the captain arrived, Harris handed him his coffee with two sugars, no cream. Just the way he liked it.

The captain looked surprised, but took a sip as he settled into his chair. "Well, we've waited 700 years for this moment—let's take a look around."

Treeha scrolled through pictures of the ship that had appeared orbiting around their sun. "The design is like nothing we've seen before," Galik, one of her lead scientists, said. "I don't think it's Ogatun."

"Why not?" Treeha asked. "They've designed strange-looking ships before."

"Well, for one, it's not armed. At least not as far as we can tell."

The ship was lovely—long and tapered, like a fish. Its surface was silvery, and marred only by what she could only assume were letters in some alien language. Unarmed aliens? It seemed like something out of a story, not anything that could actually happen.

"If that's the case, then we'd better get someone out there to protect them before the Ogatun find them and use them for target practice. But proceed with caution, they might have weapons we can't detect."

"Understood, General."

"Has someone informed my mother? She'll want to be the one to make contact."

"Yes, the Queen has been informed. She seems cautiously optimistic about the situation."

"Then I will endeavor to be the same."

Her tablet dinged. The cheerful sound made her scowl. It was time for her weekly chat with her sisters. They would insist that she look at their pups, as if exposure could suddenly make her long for offspring of her own. They would chatter about their mates or their potential mates, Liana would still be moping, and Treeha would have nothing to contribute to the conversation.

It wasn't that she didn't love her sisters. She did. She just wished that she had a single thing in common with any of them.

She had no interest in potential mates. She didn't even have any close friendships. She was too busy with her work. Which she cared deeply about, but none of her sisters cared to hear about.

There would be time for friendships and even romance later, when one of her sisters finally replaced her, when she could no longer serve her purpose.

The ship had held up admirably during the crew's 700 year slumber, thanks to Alice's careful care. "We're right where we wanted to be, sir," Lieutenant Cole, the navigation officer, said. Excitement crept into her voice. "Scans show signs of civilization on the fourth planet. I'm picking up—"

"Sir," Ensign Fisher, the communications officer, interrupted, "we're being hailed."

Captain Phillips took a deep breath. "Well, then. We prepped for this. Remember, everyone. We are the new kids in town, and we don't want to be seen as invaders. We need to make a good first impression." He looked around, meeting everyone on the bridge crew's eyes before nodding once. "Open the channel."

An unfamiliar language greeted their ears. The universal translator usually only needed a few words before it started working, but apparently the new galaxy had some new phonetic rules.

"I believe that they're trying to also broadcast visually, but our systems seem incompatible," Fisher said.

"Do what you can." The captain handed Harris his empty mug. Harris took the mug back to the wall unit and got himself a mint tea. His stomach was a little unsettled, and he was hoping it would help.

After a few minutes, the viewing screen crackled to frizzy life, and Fisher let out a tiny cheer. The image wavered, then resolved into an alien face. Large black eyes dominated a face with no nose or ears, and a wide, lipless mouth. Tiny, iridescent green-blue scales covered its skin, and a dark blue frill started on its forehead and vanished behind its head.

"They're fish people," Lieutenant Milton, the security officer, observed.

The captain shot him an unimpressed look.

The alien repeated the same phrase a few times. It was impossible to tell if it was getting frustrated—it didn't have any facial expressions that Harris could read. After another few minutes, the screen flashed, and a diagram replaced the alien's face.

"That looks like a flight plan," Cole said.

The captain stood. "Well, if they're inviting us down, we should probably go. Fisher, Milton, and McMillan, you're all with me."

Harris's stomach still felt off, and his head was starting to swim in a really unsettling way. He wasn't sure if he was up for first contact less than an hour after coming out of cold sleep.

But the captain smiled and clapped him on the shoulder. "AIs are a kind of alien intelligence, right? I'm counting on your unique point of view."

Treeha tried to put the alien spaceship out of her mind. If it wasn't a threat, it wasn't her responsibility. She was a General, not the Queen. But it was exciting. Proof that life, intelligent life, existed on other planets. And it had apparently come in peace.

Leepra, her second-in-command, entered her tent and crossed her arms over her chest. "The Ogatun are on the move."

"Have they noticed our visitors?"

"Not as far as we can tell. But they are gathering forces outside the western current. Just on their side of the border, of course."

"I'm sure they will call it some kind of scientific study or environmental survey if we question them. Amass some of our forces nearby, just in case they try anything. But don't draw any forces from the capital, just in case this is a ploy and they did notice our guests."

Leepra ruffled her frill. "As you say."

Treeha's communication pad beeped. For a moment, she considered ignoring it. But she knew better. One didn't ignore a call from the Queen. "Hi, mother."

"You could have come to visit after your rest. You didn't need to return directly to the front. Leepra is able to see to things in your absence, you know."

"I prefer to be here, just in case."

"The Ogatun wouldn't issue another challenge so soon, and even if they did, courtesy dictates that they wait for you to arrive. You can take a vacation every once in a while."

Visiting her mother was not Treeha's idea of a vacation, but she knew better than to say so.

"Liana is inconsolable. It wouldn't have killed you to spend a little more time with her. She thinks that you're heartbroken."

"I'm not."

Her mother blinked both sets of eyelids. "Oh, I know. But someday, someone else will be able to replace you, and you'll have to accept it."

"When it happens, I will accept it. I refuse to worry about it before I must."

"And you will choose a mate and exchange soulflowers and hatch a brood of your own. You are too gifted not to pass your talents along."

15

Treeha made a noncommittal noise. She knew she should want those things, but the thought of binding herself to someone, of spending all of her time caring for a clutch of eggs, of having to raise hatchlings—it all sounded both onerous and dull. And who would love her, when she didn't long for the things that everyone else did?

"No one can stay frozen in one stage forever, Treeha. You must step from General to Mother."

"I know," she said, feeling broken and alone, and wishing that she'd never confessed her feelings to her mother. But maybe the Ogatun would kill her and none of it would be her problem anymore.

She couldn't remember the last time the Ogatun had killed a single Argillan, let alone a General. But still. It wasn't impossible.

Her mother gave her one last long look, then mercifully changed the subject. "The aliens are on their way down. Their language is strange. And they are incredibly ugly. Pink and dull and covered with some kind of fuzz. I'll be meeting with them shortly."

"You've seen them?"

"They transmitted video, along with some incomprehensible audio. They seem able to follow a flight plan, at least."

Treeha suddenly wished that she had stayed in the capitol a little longer. "Be careful."

"I always am."

The shuttle ride down to the surface did nothing to settle Harris's stomach, and his head started aching when they stepped out into the alien air. The sun was bluer than Earth's and the sky brighter. The landing area was a small flat area on a rocky volcanic island. Flowers and scrubby grass clung in tiny sheltered patches between craggy rocks, and a few pale, coral-like plants grew in patches. The land-coral barely reached Harris's shoulder, but were the tallest plants in view.

The air smelled like the ocean, with just a hint of something sharp and sweet, like citrus. A few deep breaths made his stomach settle, but his head still felt fuzzy.

The planet was mostly shallow water, but there were thousands of scattered volcanic islands and a handful of places where the ocean floor dropped away. Their preliminary scans had shown that the aliens seemed to split their time between the land and water, and had built sprawling cities that crossed coastal boundaries as if they meant nothing.

Harris tried to make scientific observations about the aliens as they escorted them toward one of their enclaves. They were bipedal and seemed, on average, to stand a little shorter than humans. They had four digits, three long, webbed fingers and an opposable thumb. They were hairless, and their shimmering scales shaded from bright blue to deep green to pale gray. The frill on their heads extended down the back of their necks and vanished beneath the knee-length toga-like garments that they all wore.

They were also armed. They all carried long tridents, and some also had long tubes that must be some kind of dart gun. He couldn't read any expressions in their faces or voices as they ushered their guests along.

Milton seemed nervous with his stiff shoulders and darting eyes. Fisher just seemed excited.

Harris couldn't read Captain Phillips any better than he could the aliens. The man appeared perfectly calm. Who knows, maybe he was.

They drew closer to the low structure that seemed to be their destination, and dizziness crashed over Harris like a wave. The world around him doubled, wavered, then settled back to normal.

Milton grabbed his arm, steadying him. "You doing okay, McMillan?"

"Just dizzy. Maybe it's the air?"

Milton frowned. "I hope not."

They kept walking. Milton dragged Harris for a few steps, then, when he didn't seem in any danger of toppling over, released him.

He fell slightly behind the rest of the group, but kept walking.

It was cool in the shelter of the building, and Harris's headache faded. Water burbled somewhere farther in, and their guides led them down a long, wide corridor.

The corridor opened into a grotto. A spring dominated the center of the space, and a stream flowed off to the left. Moss glowed on the cave walls, illuminating the whole space with a gentle blue-green light. An alien sat on the edge of the spring, its bare dangling legs in the water.

The air smelled of mud and damp, but a faint breeze carried the scent of flowers.

The rest of the group gathered around the spring and attempted to communicate, but Harris hung back, observing. The guards ignored him, focusing on the alien sitting in the spring. Fisher was talking and fiddling with her portable translator. The alien seemed to be trying to tell them something in gestures.

The scent of flowers called to him.

He remembered the cherry blossoms. He wanted to see what the flowers on this planet looked like.

Sneaking off was a terrible idea. In a corner of his mind, his common sense screamed at him, appalled that he'd even consider something so foolish. Still, he took one step back, then another.

No one noticed him. Which was odd, really. Someone should be noticing him. Why weren't they?

Was he invisible? Maybe he'd passed out, and this was all a strange dream.

He felt distant and unconnected, like something else was moving his body. It should have been frightening, but he felt at peace. Like he was just where he was meant to be. If it was a dream, it was a pleasant enough one.

He found a garden. Purple and white and pink and yellow flowers filled the space, covering every inch of the craggy rock around the smooth stone path. The only light came from the moss on the walls—how did flowers grow here, with no sunlight?

"What a strange garden," he murmured, and his voice echoed. All of the flowers were beautiful and unique. Then he spotted it. The most beautiful flower that he'd ever seen—a pale pink blossom nestled in the darkest corner. It was just the color of that cherry blossom petal, back on earth, the one that had fallen into his coffee. He picked his way over to it, careful not to step on any of the other flowers.

He reached down and touched one of the flower's petals. It reminded him of a tulip, but it was more open, like a star. It smelled like strawberries and moonlight.

The stem was pulpy and green, and broke easily. He made his way back to the path, clutching the flower to his chest, feeling disconnected and dreamy.

He wandered back the way he came, till he met one of the guards, striding toward him, her frill curled in fury. "What are you doing here?" she demanded, clutching her trident tight.

"I'm not sure," he said. "I feel strange."

The guard noticed the flower in his hand. "Did you pick that?" she asked.

He blinked twice, looked down at the flower in his hand, nodded. "I had to."

"You felt a compulsion?"

"Yes," he said, relieved that she understood.

"And now you understand me," she said in a tone of sudden realization. "And can even speak."

He blinked at her. "That does seem odd, now that you mention it."

"Who is your soul bound to?" the guard asked.

"Treeha la llaa vo Blumdar." He smiled as he spoke the name, and felt a sudden pull, like something had tied a fishing line around his soul.

The guard lowered her trident and crossed her arms over her chest. "I should take you to the Queen, my Prince."

"I feel very odd," Harris said. "I think I need to sit down before I fall over."

Treeha knew the very instant that her soulflower was plucked. She was in the middle of a tactical breakdown of the threat at the western current, and the world around her went wavy.

She'd heard stories of the heartpull, but had thought they were just that. Stories. Things people exaggerated for dramatic interest. But she felt a physical pull deep in her chest. Taking a step away from the pull was painful, moving toward it right and comforting, like stepping into the ocean after a long dry walk.

That she could feel such a strong tug so far from the capital could only mean that whoever had claimed her soulflower had felt the compulsion to do so.

The compulsion was a thing of fairy tales, of girlish daydreams. It wasn't something that actually happened. Certainly not something that happened to someone like her.

She suffered through the rest of the meeting, only just able to pay attention. "I need to return to the capital," she said as soon as the meeting finally ended.

Leepra looked alarmed. "Why?"

"Someone picked my soulflower."

"Who would dare? Surely none of the Ogatun could penetrate our defenses to steal your bond, and none of our people would do so without your consent."

"It is one of the aliens. He felt the compulsion."

"An alien? How?"

Treeha shook her head. She was starting to feel frantic to reach his side. Harris McMillan, her soulmate. He needed her. "I don't know how. I have to go."

Treeha's communication pad dinged. "Hello mother," she said.

"One of the aliens picked your soulflower."

"I know. His name is Harris McMillan."

"So he really did feel the compulsion. The guard who found him said he spoke our language before he passed out. I need you here."

"I'm already on my way."

Harris woke in a simple but comfortable room. Smooth stone was softened by pillows stuffed with dried seaweed and lit by more of that glowing moss. He was curled up against one wall, as close to the pull in his heart as he could manage.

The rest of the landing party were all sitting on a long bench built into the opposite room, staring at him.

"What the hell is going on, McMillan?" Captain Phillips demanded.

Harris tried to focus, but Treeha was coming, and he could feel her moving. She was so far away, so absurdly far, but she was approaching, and quickly.

"I'm honestly not sure, sir."

"One of the guards carried you in, clutching a flower, and the whole place exploded in an uproar. They took the flower and bundled us in here."

"It needs to be stored safely till it sublimates," he said. Still, he missed the soft pink shade, the subtle scent. "I wish they'd left it."

"What needs to be stored safely?" Milton demanded.

"Treeha's soulflower." It seemed unfair that he didn't have a soulflower that she could pick. But the bond seemed complete without it.

His crewmates were staring. "Did you just say something in their language?" Fisher asked.

"Did I?" Harris frowned. The two languages flowed together in his mind. One was his, and one was Treeha's, but he and Treeha were one, so of course he knew both of them. He tried again. "The soulflower. Was that in English?"

"What the fresh hell is a soulflower?" Milton asked.

"And how the hell are you speaking their language at all?" Fisher asked.

The captain held up his hands. "I think McMillan is just as confused as the rest of us. Maybe more so."

"If we find more of these flowers, can we learn the language, too?" Fisher asked.

"No!" Harris stood up, horror suffusing his whole body. "No, absolutely not, what a horrible question."

Fisher sneered. "So it's okay for you to do it, but no one else can?"

"I felt the compulsion."

"Speak English!" Fisher snapped.

"I couldn't help it. It was fate. Destiny. I was only completing a connection that was forged long before either of us were born. Just wandering in and taking a soulflower at random is a horrible violation. They can only be taken with the consent of both parties, or through the compulsion."

"Are you really telling us that you have a magical bond with some fish-woman alien that you could only meet because you traveled through space for 700 years?" Milton asked.

Harris collapsed onto the bed. What an overwhelming question. What if he hadn't come? Would she have eventually bonded to someone else?

But it didn't matter. He had come. He was here, and she was on her way.

"And you believe that she's your... soulmate?" Fisher asked.

Harris nodded.

The captain leaned forward. "More importantly, is that what the aliens believe? It was hard to tell, but I think they seemed upset. They didn't threaten us, but they didn't give us any choice about coming in here, either."

"I can ask," Harris said, levering himself back onto his feet. There was a panel next to the closed door, and he reached toward it.

"Don't bother," Milton said. "It doesn't do anything."

Harris placed his palm against the panel and closed his eyes. Treeha's people could control the electrical currents in their bodies, and that was how they used these panels.

A spark flashed between him and the panel, and the door opened, but he flinched back, shaking his now-numb hand. "Ouch."

"What did you do?"

Harris opened his mouth, closed it, and then shook his head.

The guard that he'd spoken to before was standing in the hall. "How can we serve you, my Prince?" she asked.

"I just wanted to know what was going on."

"The General is on her way at all speed. She should be here by sundown."

Harris smiled and rubbed his chest, where he still felt the pull. "And my companions?"

"We were unsure what you wished for them. Do you have orders?"

"Maybe some refreshments?"

"It will be done."

"Are they free to leave if they wish?"

"Yes, of course."

"Thank you. What is your name?"

"Gladola."

"Thank you, Gladola. You have been a great help."

He turned back to the captain. "I asked her to bring some refreshments, in case you're hungry or anything, and she says you're free to go, if you want."

"I'm not going anywhere," Fisher said. "You're going to teach me this language."

"We'll all stay," Captain Phillips said. "It's not my habit to leave a man behind."

Treeha was relieved when Harris regained consciousness. But the pure volume of his memories was staggering, and whatever method of storage and organization that his people used was incomprehensible. It seemed almost like there was no method, like his species just kept all of their memories without any sort of archiving or recovery matrix, like it was all random and organic as a coral reef.

Treeha tried to meditate, but she was too excited to clear her mind.

When she was very young, she'd daydreamed that someone might feel the compulsion and pluck her soulflower, that she would be connected to another being, mind to mind, heart to heart, soul to soul. But as she'd grown older, she'd given the dream up. Whose soul could possibly fit with hers? Her, with her broken, incomplete heart. Her, who felt nothing but dread at the prospect of becoming a Mother someday.

But now, there was someone who could know her and love her completely.

Someone with whom she could never be expected to raise a clutch.

Someone who would allow her to be a General forever and never a Mother or a Queen.

Harris McMillian was a gift beyond her wildest hopes.

The hours dragged, but eventually her train arrived at the capital.

Her mother, bless her for her kindness and foresight, had brought him to the station.

He stood with a cluster of other aliens. Humans, they called themselves. They were all wearing the same strange clothing that clung to their bodies like a second skin. They were strange to look at—the bond supplied words for things like 'hair' and 'pants' but she had never seen them with her own eyes before.

She knew which of the strange figures was Harris immediately. He broke away from the rest and ran toward her, and she found herself running, too.

She threw herself into his arms, and he caught her and spun her around, laughing.

It was a strange sound, his laughter. Unlike anything she'd ever heard before.

He placed her carefully back on her feet and leaned his forehead against hers. "That's better," he said.

"Agreed." The pull was finally gone. They were together. Where they belonged. "It is good to meet you, Harris."

"You as well, Treeha."

His companions approached. "Well, that was certainly dramatic," one of them said.

"You should not judge feelings beyond your ken," Treeha said.

"Oh, you speak our language, too!" Treeha tried to sort through Harris's memories for the talkative one's name, but they were all an absurd tangle.

"I do. I will aid you and negotiate on behalf of my people so that we may continue on in peaceful relations. But first, I would like some time alone with my soulmate."

"You both really believe all that junk about soulmates and fated romance, huh? Even after seeing each other?"

Harris threaded his fingers through hers. "You can't argue that we're not connected, Milton," he said. "We learned each other's language in an instant, and Fisher can't even get the translator to grasp basic sentence structure."

Fisher, the talkative one, Milton, the doubtful one. Treeha made a note in her memory. It was only polite to remember her soulmate's friends. She tugged at Harris's arm.

"We'll be back shortly, Captain," he said, nodding to one of the men who hadn't spoken.

"Apparently it's your honeymoon, but do remember that we can't communicate without you."

"Of course, sir."

Treeha kept a small room in the capital, tucked up against her mother's and sisters' more spacious quarters.

As soon as the door slid shut behind them, Harris wrapped his arms around her, and they stood there, quietly soaking in each other's presence.

"Your mind is a staggering tangle," she said, eventually.

She felt his smile. It was such a strange thing, a smile. Flashing teeth to show happiness. And he was so warm, his skin so water-smooth, without the comforting scrape of scales.

"We don't order our minds as you do."

"Appalling, how do you remember anything?" she murmured.

He laughed. "It's not always easy. But I can try your way, if you can show me how."

"Close your eyes and clear your mind."

They sank into meditation together. She could feel how they'd altered each other already—he already had some rudimentary control over his electrical field, and she could feel that her own memory matrix had expanded—she could store more memories than she'd ever dreamed necessary. And more changes would come, she was sure. The thought should have been terrifying, but instead it was a comfort. She and Harris were so different, but they would grow toward each other, be each other's reflection.

They sorted through his memories together, smoothing out tangles, finding places for facts that he often needed but could never remember.

She learned the shape of him, this man who was her other half. He was kind and patient, gentle and considerate. Always concerned with the feelings of others, especially those who everyone else discounted.

There was a shadowy, jagged shape that hurt him when she prodded it.

"That's Roxanne. My ex."

She took a moment to understand. A former lover. Someone he'd cared about before he met her.

She felt a surge of jealousy. It was not a feeling she was much acquainted with, and she did not like it.

"She's dead," he said. "She's been dead for centuries."

"Then you have no need of these memoires. Delete them."

She felt his spike of alarm. "Humans don't delete memories just because we don't need them."

Treeha's jealousy curled tight in her chest. "I have had no loves before you."

"Not even any that you've forgotten?"

"No." She probed the memory again. "She hurt you. Why do you want to hold onto this?"

Harris bowed his head. "This is important to you, isn't it? That I let her go? That I forget?"

"Yes. I wouldn't ask you if it wasn't."

He thought for a moment. She could sense his struggle. She tried to remember how she'd felt when deleting her first memory, the trepidation and childish worry that she might someday need it. "I will not force you," she said. "If you truly want to keep these memories, that is your choice."

Eventually, he nodded. "Okay. Okay. Show me how."

The memories contained strange barbs, but those vanished as they went through, erasing the other woman's face from his mind.

There were other dark memories. His people had been at war, a bitter and violent conflict made all the more tragic by their failed attempts to avoid it.

For all of her years of war, she had never killed anyone. Harris had.

These memories hurt him, too. "These are important," Harris said.

Treeha squeezed his hands. "Yes."

"I feel lighter without those other memories," he said, smiling. "Like I was sick, and you were the cure."

"Thank you for being willing to do it. And for being willing to reorder your mind so that I could better understand you. You have done more for me than I have for you."

He pulled her back into his arms. "You respected my choices. That is all I'd ask for."

She had never enjoyed physical contact before. With him, it was different. She felt comfort without judgment, support without demands.

"We should probably get back to my crew."

"You are a Prince among my people, now. I don't like that you have to take orders from your Captain Phillips."

"Well, I'll need training to be worthy to stand by your side. I should probably request a leave of absence from my duties once Fisher gets the translator set."

"I continue to ask for more than I give."

He shook his head. "No. Even though I don't remember the cause, I know I was hurt and betrayed. Helping me deal with all of that is amazing."

"It won't all be easy," she warned. "I am difficult to love. Even my mother says so."

She knew that they should go through her memories, so he could know her as she knew him. But she was worried that he might not like what he saw. Her stubbornness, her temper, her lack of interests beyond her duty. How petty the war she'd devoted her life to seemed in comparison to the one his people had worked so hard to avoid. She let the moment slip away.

Harris laughed and hugged her tighter. "We're soulmates, stop fretting."

Harris could feel the gaps in his memory, like empty spaces on a full bookshelf.

It had been strange, moving his memories around in his mind like files on a computer. He'd always felt more akin to computers than people, and now his mind almost worked like an AI. He'd have to talk to Alice about it. He was sure she would have valuable insight into editable memory.

Treeha had been so cute, sulking about his past romance. The look on her face when he'd agreed to delete his memories was something he'd treasure forever.

And the moment that she'd assured him that the choice was his alone. He had the sense that his choices hadn't always been his own, in the past.

He felt lighter without his baggage. Like he'd taken everything toxic that he'd been holding onto and fired it into the sun.

He'd traveled for 700 years and countless miles, and it was Treeha who'd truly let him let his past go.

He couldn't stop smiling.

Treeha was meeting with Captain Phillips and her mother, the Queen, working out details about where the humans could settle.

He was with Milton and Fisher. He was trying to help the communications officer with the fundamentals of Treeha's language. Milton was reading something on his communication pad and occasionally chuckling.

Fisher seemed nearly ready to throw the portable translator against the wall in frustration. "It's not fair! Why did you get the magic mind transference? I'm the communications officer, I should be the one who can talk to them!"

"You're not the one with the destiny," Milton said, not looking up from his book.

"I could have a destiny," Fisher snapped. "Maybe it's not to be instantly in love with a fish-person, but I'm okay with that."

"Do you actually find her attractive?" Fisher asked. "Like, do you want to—"

"Oh, shut up, now I'm picturing it," Milton said.

"You are both incredibly unprofessional," Harris said.

"I think it's perfectly normal to be curious," Fisher said. "I mean, this is first contact. And maybe you two are having your own private first contact."

Milton snickered at the word 'private.'

Harris sighed. "I've never really been attracted to anyone in the way you mean," he said. "I'm asexual."

Milton sat up, his book forgotten. "Wait, what? I heard you were essentially Captain Berry's love slave."

There was that gap in his memory. "Our relationship was complicated," he said, trusting that that was at least mostly true.

"Complicated, huh? Sounds like she was abusing her position of power to me," Milton said. "I always thought she seemed shady."

Harris didn't want to get into the whole memory-erasure thing with these two. Not now, at least. They might be friends eventually, but they weren't yet. "Well, I got away from her. And now I'm here, where I belong."

Milton shook his head. "Do you feel like you joined some kind of cult? Cause you kind of sound like it. You just believe in their weird flower magic so completely."

"I've always believed in fate."

"So, you don't really feel desire, what about her? How does that work?" Fisher asked.

"They don't have a sex drive. They breed like some fish on earth—the woman lays unfertilized eggs and her partner fertilizes them afterwards."

"Is it weird to have your head suddenly so packed full of new knowledge?" Milton asked. "It sounds super confusing."

"Sort of? We did a bunch of meditating together, and that helped."

"Argh, I'm just so jealous!" Fisher said. She fiddled with the translator. "Still it's interesting that they are so different from us, but they still meditate," Fisher said. "I wonder if that means something."

"Either way, we're off topic. Aren't we supposed to be recording verbs in various tenses?" Harris said, very much not wanting to get into how differently Treeha's mind, and now his, worked from how theirs did.

Fisher sighed. "You're right. It's just frustrating. I'm usually almost as good as the translator, and I am just not getting this language."

"You'll get it. I'm proof that human minds can grasp it, at least."

"But is your mind purely human?" Milton asked. "You have a psychic bond with an alien."

Harris was very glad that he hadn't mentioned the memory-rearranging. He ignored Milton and started listing verbs again.

Harris respected this Captain Phillips, and Treeha could see why. He was smart and forthright.

"We have a small crew of 150 individuals now, but we have a whole colony's worth of frozen embryos so that we can create a self-sustaining population. Of course, we didn't know there was another civilization here when we set out. We do ask that you allow us to settle here with you, but I understand if you are hesitant to grant that request."

"You brought my daughter's soulmate, so there must be some destiny involved in your presence," the Queen said. "We will allow you to settle. There is an island chain near the center of our territory that we have very little use for."

"Your territory?" Captain Phillips asked.

"We are at war with another faction," Treeha said.

"Do you have need of a diplomat? I'd be happy to offer my services to broker peace."

Treeha was aghast at the suggestion. She wasn't even sure how to translate it. "We appreciate the offer," Treeha said after a long moment, "but our conflict is not something that can be resolved."

"Any conflict can be resolved."

"We have no desire for peace with the Ogatun," she said. "And they have no desire for peace with us. But our conflict with them is not like the war your people experienced. It is not something you need to worry about."

Captain Phillips' bumpy face twisted in a way that she couldn't quite read, but he let the matter drop, and Treeha went back to her role as translator.

"We'll get to work on the island chain that you have offered," he said. "Can you give us a safe flight plan to arrive there?"

"Of course," Treeha's mother said. "And now we must speak of our new Prince. I understand that he has a duty to your people, but he is soulmate to our General, and must receive appropriate training."

"I can temporarily release him from his current duties, and he can be the official human envoy to the general."

Treeha didn't like that Harris was only 'temporarily' released from his duties, but it was better than nothing. He could begin his training. Negotiations continued, and Treeha continued translating, but there was nothing else she was invested in. She had what she wanted, after all.

Harris returned to the ship to gather his personal belongings. "I am going to go train," he said to Alice as he packed. "I'm a little nervous."

"Your new people seem very logical. The way that you describe the workings of their minds is fascinating. And the soulflowers are lovely. They remind me of something from a particularly fanciful breed of fanfiction. But I don't understand their insistence on their endless war."

"It's part of their culture. They don't really have battles or anything. The Generals fight, and the winner demands some concessions from the loser."

"Does anyone die in this so-called war?"

"When they do have battles, they take prisoners that are later exchanged. There are some accidents. Sometimes a youth won't surrender when they should. But it's rare. It's more like a sporting event than a real war."

"So they have a sort of play-war that they continue to enact. Why?"

"Well, the Ogatun are terrible."

Alice laughed. "I'm sure they say the same about your people."

"The Argillan."

"So they are divided into the Ogatun and the Argillan. What is their word for their species as a whole?"

Harris blinked, considering the question. "I don't think they have one."

"Then I guess it's no wonder that they refused Captain Phillips' offer to broker a peace."

Harris snorted. Peace with the Ogatun. What an absurd notion. Then he stopped. Humans believed in peace, in talking out issues and burying the hatchet.

Though it was hard to be passionate about ending Treeha's war when it was less deadly than most popular sports on Earth. Still, the fact that it was bloodless now didn't mean it would stay that way.

"I think Fisher and Milton are right, I have joined a cult."

"Well, take one of my communicators with you, and I'll be happy to talk with you anytime you feel like you need some outside perspective."

"Thanks, Alice."

Treeha presented Harris to the elders who had trained her. "He is precious to me, and fragile," she said. "You must forge him into a weapon."

"I'm not sure I want to be a weapon," Harris murmured.

She squeezed his hand, again feeling some guilt for asking so much of him. But she was a General, she needed her soulmate to be able to fight—the Ogatun General could challenge him in her place. But she would not force him—the memories that they'd deleted together held too much of him feeling powerless in his own life. "If you would rather I protect you, I can do my best." She imagined an Ogatun standing over him, trident raised, and pushed the image away.

Harris took a deep breath. "No. You're right. I want to learn to defend myself as your people do, you can't be worrying about me all of the time."

"It will be a positive experience, I promise you."

Harris turned toward her and rested his forehead against hers. "I trust you."

Treeha hoped that he was right to.

***

Harris had been training for three days, and he wasn't sure if he was going to be drowned or electrocuted first.

The ancient fish-men who were in charge of his training didn't share their names with him, and he couldn't find them in Treeha's memories either.

He was exhausted and sore, and they kept demanding impossible things.

But he kept managing them. It was in turns frustrating and exhilarating.

"You will need to learn to breathe water if you are ever going to earn your place at the General's side," one said.

"Humans don't breathe water," Harris said, gasping from the countless laps they'd just made him swim.

"You will," another of the ancients said.

***

Treeha swam back and forth, trying to push herself to the same level of physical exhaustion that she felt from Harris. She felt waves of anger and despair, and anticipated him giving up during every moment of the day.

She was a monster for forcing all this on him. Surely he'd grow to hate her.

She was allowed only one visit per week, and approached each one cautiously, expecting that this would be the time he turned away from her.

But he always smiled and held her, even when he could hardly lift his arms. He'd lean his forehead against hers and say, "That's better," and her heart melted every time.

She could see the physical changes in him, from week to week. Scales clustered between his fingers, webbing grew between his toes, and gills opened beneath his ribs. His brown eyes shaded just a bit darker, closer to the black of her own.

"I finally managed to create a charge underwater without knocking myself out," he said. "And look, they gave me a present."

It was a heavy metal rod, just longer than his hand, strung on a braided cord and hung around his neck. He tugged it off of the cord, then shook it. It telescoped and bloomed into a lightweight trident. He shook it again and it shrank back to a simple rod.

"It is a fine present."

"I have one for you, too." He pressed a seashell into her hand. "They were having me meditate on the ocean floor, and I found this there. It reminded me of your soulflower."

It was a soft pink, as she knew her soulflower had been, and the shape was almost right. And these shells tended to gather on ledges far deeper than he could have reached just a week ago.

"Why are you pushing yourself so hard?" she asked.

"I'm not the one doing the pushing!" he protested. "It's those old men."

"They only push you as hard as you wish them to. It is their way."

They were quiet long enough that she didn't think he'd answer. But then he pushed both hands through his hair and let out a frustrated huff. "I've always been weak. I'm tired of it. I've never succeeded at goals that I thought were impossible before. But now—I can breathe underwater. My body changed because I willed it. And because of you, and our connection. If it's possible, I owe it to you to do it, don't I? My destiny is finally in front of me, I can't ignore it."

"What do your people do to train? You keep moving toward me, but I should move toward you, too. I can't remain a stationary target."

"You have your duties."

"I can take a vacation."

"Are you sure? You've never taken a vacation."

"Then it's past time, isn't it?"

He smiled at her. "Maybe you could go visit the human colony and ask Milton for some human-style training."

She nodded. "I will."

Treeha had spent more time on dry land than many of her people, but she had never jogged before.

It was a horrible activity. It made her lungs burn in a most unpleasant way, and the impact made her knees ache. But then she thought about the pain Harris had felt when his gills had opened up, and she shook her head at her own weakness.

Milton seemed to take much greater delight in her misery than the ancients had ever shown. "Two more laps!" he shouted, when by her count she should be done.

She finally finished and collapsed in the scant shade under a spiney land coral. Her breath came in ragged pants.

Milton stretched out next to her. "So, you're training in our way since McMillan is training in yours?"

She nodded. "He's finished the physical conditioning, next up is the combat training."

"Huh, McMillan in hand-to-hand combat. That's something I'd like to see."

"He will issue a challenge to the Ogatun General when he is ready, your people are welcome to observe the bout."

"Wait, you're going to have him fight in your war? But he's not involved in that!"

"Of course he is, he is my soulmate."

"What if this Ogatun guy kills him?"

"The fight is not to the death. I also expect him to win. This General has yet to defeat me. He is not a good fighter. He prefers words to actions."

"Sounds reasonable enough to me."

"He is a coward who deserves to be wiped from his own mother's memory."

"If you say so. You recovered? Ready for some lunges?"

Treeha groaned, but did as he demanded.

Harris stood on a high cliff, looking down at the waves crashing against the rocks hundreds of feet below.

"This is the last test," one of the ancients said. He held a pearl out over the ledge and let it drop. Harris watched it till it grew too small to see, long before it hit the water with an invisible splash.

Then he dove after it.

Air rushed by faster and faster, and still he plummeted. His hands held overhead, his chin tucked. He hit the water with a crushing impact that he hardly registered.

He pushed himself deeper and deeper, pulling water into his still-unfamiliar gills. He plunged past silvery fish and cloud-like sea fungus. He felt the pressure growing as the water grew cold and dark around him.

He swam as the pressure built to pain, then past it. When he could no longer see with his eyes, he reached out with his electrical field. It sparked around him. His skin was too numb from the cold to register the charge of it.

After what seemed an eternity of motion, he sensed the pearl, resting on the rocky bottom.

He grasped it and pushed back up toward the light.

When he surfaced, the ancients were gone, their job done. He floated for a bit before he dragged himself into the boat they'd left anchored for him.

The pearl fit perfectly into the hilt of his telescoping trident.

Treeha would be proud of him.

But more importantly, he was proud of himself.

Treeha slumped at a table and poked at the hot goop that humans called food. Her people ate fish and seaweed and sometimes had sweet fruits that grew in the shallows as a treat. They didn't heat their food. Humans had so many textures and flavors and shapes in their food. It was unnecessary and exhausting.

As was their insistence on communal eating. Her people ate when it was necessary. Alone. They did not make meals into some kind of group bonding.

Fisher plopped down next to her. "How's the stew?"

"Warm," Treeha said, poking it again.

Milton joined them, followed by Cole, who's just come down from the ship in orbit.

"How is McMillan holding up?" Milton asked. "He's starting his combat training, right? And your weekly visit is soon?"

"Yes, tomorrow. He's done very well, the ancients are impressed."

Fisher sighed. "Getting trained by mysterious ancients, now. Just add that to the checklist of cool things McMillan gets to do."

"We do cool stuff, too," Cole said. "We're still farther away from Earth than any other humans before."

"Yippee," Fisher said.

"Why did you all decide to come here? I know why Harris joined this mission, but what about the rest of you?" Treeha asked.

The humans exchanged a look that she couldn't read.

"Well, I came for adventure," Fisher said. "New place, hopefully new people. A whole new language, something that the translator can't just handle."

Cole reached out and took Fisher's hand. "And you got all that." She smiled at Treeha. "I came because she did. Couldn't let her leave me behind."

Milton rubbed the back of his neck. "I just didn't have any reason to stay. Lost everyone in the war. I needed a fresh start."

Fisher and Cole reached out and each took one of his hands, so they formed a tiny closed circle. Milton smiled up at them. "I guess I got what I was looking for, too."

Fisher stood up. "Come on, guys, bring it in. Group hug."

And so Treeha found herself dragged into their group embrace. It was just as warm as the stew. But much nicer.

Harris tapped into Treeha's memories to help with his combat training. It felt like cheating at first, but as Leepra threw more and more opponents against him, he needed every advantage he could grasp.

He fought and he swam and he practiced throwing lightning without hurting himself. Days slipped into weeks into months. Treeha complained about Milton's sadistic streak and Fisher's invasive questions, but he knew that she enjoyed their company. They were certainly more friendly than Leepra, who treated Harris with the same distant reverence she held Treeha in.

He and Treeha could sense each other's thoughts when they meditated, which helped with the lonely hours after training was done. He also spent a lot of time talking to Alice, who was monitoring both the ship and the brand-new colony.

The psychic bond was a comfort, but only getting to see Treeha once a week was painful, and he tried his best to spend what time they had wisely.

Her time training had altered her, just like his had, though her physical changes weren't as drastic as new gills. The shape of her legs changed and her chest cavity expanded with her increased lung capacity.

She examined herself in the mirror when he pointed out the changes. "It's only fair, you are greatly changed." She traced the scales that glittered between his fingers. "Your changes are far more obvious."

"I was worried about my hair, but it seems to be sticking around, thank goodness."

Treeha ran her fingers through his hair, apparently enjoying the springy feel of it. "It would probably make swimming easier."

"Hush."

"I confess, I am glad that I haven't sprouted any."

He laughed, and they sat together in silence for a few moments. "Leepra says that I should be ready to issue my challenge soon."

"Milton wants to come watch."

"That's embarrassing."

"Our whole army will be watching."

"But they're watching for you, not me. If any humans come, I can't pretend they don't care about me." He also wasn't looking forward to their reactions to his changed body. He hadn't suggested that he come to the colony instead of having Treeha journey to him to avoid the unwanted attention.

"I can forbid it, if you wish. But Milton will pout, and Fisher will never let it go. She'll add it to her list."

Harris sighed. "No, they can come. I'll have to face them eventually."

Treeha always felt calm before her own bouts, but she couldn't wrestle down a choking anxiety as Harris strode into the arena.

"Holy shit," Fisher said. "That's McMillan?"

"Who else would it be?" Treeha asked.

"He's super ripped. What have you people had him doing?"

"Swimming and fighting, mostly."

"I suppose that would do it," Milton said.

"Do we cheer?" Fisher asked.

"You may."

Fisher grinned and stood, cupping her hands around her mouth. "Go McMillan! Kick his ass!" Then she let out a strange wooping sound, which made Treeha's people wince.

The Ogatun General entered the arena. "Is that the bad guy?" Fisher asked.

"Yes."

"Booooo!" she shouted. "You're going down, fish-guy!"

Treeha was glad that none of her own people understood Fisher's weak insults, but she couldn't help smiling. Which would be another thing her people wouldn't understand.

Harris stood and faced his opponent. Treeha couldn't hear them from where she sat with the humans, but she could see the Ogatun's mouth moving.

She felt a wave of amusement from Harris, then he moved. He swept the Ogatun's legs as he spun and landed a sharp blow to his torso.

"Ooh, he's winning!" Fisher said.

"That was a solid move," Milton said.

The fight continued below them. Harris's style was different from Treeha's—she preferred a single blow to finish the combat, while Harris hit his opponent again and again.

The Ogatun General backed off and started talking again. But this time it was clearly a ploy—Treeha could see electricity sparking down his arm, but the bulk of his body hid it from Harris's sight.

"Is his arm sparking?" Fisher asked, frantic. "Is he going to throw lightning? I thought you said Harris wouldn't die, even if he lost?"

"He won't."

"Our physiology is different from yours! A shock like that could stop his heart!"

The General threw his bolt.

And Harris caught it in the tines of his trident, spun around, and sent it back, now half again as large.

The General flew backwards out of the ring, and the crowd roared its approval.

"How did he do that?" Fisher asked. Milton just gaped.

"Training," Treeha said, though she knew that was not all it was. It was also the magic of their connection.

"You're smiling," Milton noted. "I didn't think your people did that."

"Both Harris and I are changed by our link."

"If he gets to throw lightning and you just learned to smile, I think you're getting the short end of the stick," Fisher said.

Treeha laughed. It felt strange in her chest, but she found she liked the sensation. "I am not sure I agree. But I must go congratulate my soulmate on his victory."

"So, she couldn't get a mate of her own species," the Ogatun General sneered, holding his side where the lightning had hit him.

"Our link summoned me across both space and time. I was on my way to her hundreds of cycles before you were even thought of."

"How very poetic."

"I think so."

"Your people have selected the wrong side of this war," he said.

"Oh? What are your moral arguments behind that statement?" Harris asked, knowing that they fought because they fought, not because of any actual differences in belief. He shoved his own memories of war back into their dark corner of his mind.

The Ogatun General blinked both eyelids at him. "Moral arguments? The Argillan are incapable of questioning their devotion to conflict. There is no arguing with them. War is the only thing they understand."

"No one has lost the war in the past century, I'm not that worried about the future. And you're the one who lost the battle today. And the last time, and the time before that, if I understand correctly."

"What has happened to her legs?" the General murmured as Harris spotted Treeha moving through the crowd. "You are both become monsters."

"I suppose you could say that," Harris agreed. "After all, she and I are both no longer what we were before. But it is destiny. If your soulflower had been meant for a human, you would be the same."

The Ogatun general's frill rippled. "None of your kind will ever come close to my soulflower."

"They will if it is your destiny. Not even the Ogatun can stand against fate."

"Close your fleshy mouth," the General said, storming away before Treeha reached them.

She looked incredibly smug, and Harris couldn't blame the Ogatun General for falling back instead of facing her.

"Well done," she said. He felt the pride and joy pulsing through her. She had been worried for him for days, and he was glad to feel happier emotions in his soulmate.

"That was awesome!" Fisher said. "I didn't know you could throw lightning! Can you teach me?"

"I don't think so."

She sighed. "Of course not."

Milton clapped him on the back. "Nice fight. You should come to the colony and teach us some of your new moves."

"I'd be happy to."

"Just not the coolest one," Fisher grumbled.

"Treeha tells me that construction is coming along well, and I heard that we might be ready to start some embryos soon. That's exciting!"

"Ugh, babies," Fisher said.

"You do not wish to procreate?" Treeha asked.

"Nope, it's not for me. Not that there's anything wrong with wanting kids, but I just don't."

"And that is your choice?"

"Of course! Do you not get a choice?"

Treeha shook her head. "One step in life must follow the next. For the Argillan royal family, we are born Princesses, then some of us become Generals. Then we must become Mothers, and then one becomes Queen.

"But you can't become a Mother now, right? You and McMillan can't breed?"

Treeha shook her head. "I never wished to become a Mother. I thought I was alone in that feeling. I am glad I am not."

Fisher frowned. "I can't believe that you're the only one of your species who doesn't want kids."

Treeha shrugged. Harris liked seeing her mimic human mannerisms. It was adorable. "I am the first to be soulbonded to a human, maybe others will follow."

"We should all go back to the colony together and have a party to celebrate McMillan's win," Milton said. "I think the captain wants to talk to you anyway. He's having some issues with the AI."

"With Alice? She didn't mention anything to me."

"Alice?"

"The AI, that's her name."

"Her?"

"That is the pronoun she requested."

"She never mentioned it," Fisher said. "I've just been calling her it! I didn't even know she had a name!"

"Well, did you ask?" Harris said.

"It didn't occur to me that I might need to."

"Do you chat with it—her—often?" Milton asked.

"Every day. We're friends. She keeps me updated on what's going on in the colony."

"Wait, she spies on us for you?"

"She just gives me general news, Milton, nothing specific."

"Sure."

Milton sighed. "That's why I don't like the idea of personalizing the AI, it makes people apt to trust them less."

"I think seeing her as an equal member of the crew would make people trust her more, not less," Fisher said.

"She's a sentient being," Harris said. "And as such, she should have a say in how she's addressed. And she kept us alive for 700 years, so we can probably trust her."

Milton sighed. "I've never thought of it like that before. You might be right."

Treeha had spent more time at the human colony than Harris had. The humans seemed used to her presence. But Harris clearly unnerved them. They stared as he passed, and whispered amongst themselves.

"I do look different," he said to her, his voice low.

"Not more different than I am."

"No, I mean I look different than I used to. My eyes, the scales. Things like that."

"Do the changes bother you?"

He shook his head.

The captain, at least, seemed to take Harris's transformation in stride. "Good to see you, McMillan. I hear you won your fight. Congratulations."

"Thank you, Sir. Milton said you were having issues with Alice?"

Captain Phillips rubbed his forehead. "Go ahead and tell him, Alice."

"The captain thinks that my long-range scanners are malfunctioning because I have picked up another ship from Earth."

"I want you to go up there and take a look, see if there are some wires crossed somehow."

"You want him to go into space?" Treeha asked. "To your unarmed ship?" She didn't like the thought of him leaving the planet. She'd been hoping they could spend some time together, now that his training was complete.

"He has duties to my crew as well as to you, general."

"I'd be happy to help out, sir," Harris said.

Of course he would. He couldn't ignore a friend in need. Treeha sighed. "One of our ships can take him up," she offered. Then at least he wouldn't be in one of the human's defenseless shuttles.

"Would you like to come along?" Harris asked. "You could see the ship."

The captain sighed. "You know, McMillan, you should probably ask for permission before inviting people onto our ship."

"Alice has been asking to meet her," Harris said.

The captain rolled his eyes. "Oh, then my permission is clearly superfluous. Have it your way. Take Milton and Fisher with you. Find out what is going on. And McMillan?"

"Yes sir?"

"I expect you to go up in uniform, not that weird toga get-up."

Harris had to get new uniforms made, since his old ones didn't fit anymore. Going back to pants felt strange, and he kept shifting on his seat, trying to get comfortable.

Milton smirked at him. "Doesn't look like you missed wearing pants."

"The togas do look comfortable," Fisher said.

"They are," Harris said, shifting again.

He held Treeha's hand as they blasted off. She had only been to space a few times—her duties usually kept her close to the front, and the Argillan didn't engage in space battles with the Ogatun. Their orbital presence was all about observation and spear-rattling.

When they arrived at the ship, they found that Alice had set the lights in the shuttle bay to a frequency that was soothing for Treeha's eyes, and Harris appreciated the welcoming gesture. "Welcome back, Harris. And it is a pleasure to welcome you aboard, General."

"Please, call me Treeha. Any friend of Harris's is a friend of mine."

"You don't find it odd to think of me as a friend?" Alice asked.

Treeha wove her fingers through Harris's. "Not at all," she said.

"Are you not going to welcome us, too?" Milton asked.

"Greetings, Lieutenant Milton. Ensign Fisher. Welcome back aboard." The AI's tone was incredibly dry, and Harris couldn't help grinning.

"I'd love to give you a tour, but the captain wants me to check things out as quickly as possible," Harris said.

"I have run a self-diagnostic three separate times. There is nothing wrong with me. There is another ship coming."

"I believe you. But it can't hurt to check."

Alice sniffed. "I managed to look after myself for 700 years."

Harris grinned. "I know. And the captain knows. He just really doesn't like the thought of another ship following after us."

The crew members who'd remained on the ship stared as Harris and Treeha walked by. Harris made a point of smiling and introducing the few he knew by name. When they arrived at the AI core, Fisher offered to give Treeha a tour while Harris worked.

Milton leaned against the doorframe while Harris fiddled with the diagnostic systems. "Don't you have something else to do?" he asked.

"Nope. I'm here as your official bodyguard. You're a foreign dignitary, now."

Harris worked in silence for a few moments, getting into a pleasant groove, skimming through lines of perfectly functional code.

"Alice doesn't seem to like me," Milton said.

"I don't dislike you, Lieutenant Milton. I care about all of the members of the Starburst crew. But we're not friends."

"Are you always listening?" Milton asked, looking uncomfortable.

"I monitor activity on the ship. And since Harris is trying to work, I thought perhaps I could step in and keep you from distracting him."

Harris sighed. "Well, now you're both distracting me."

Milton sighed. "It's easier to deal with you watching all of the time if I don't think of you as a person. Who could be judging me."

"I can observe without passing judgment."

"Can you? Can any sentient being?"

"What are you so afraid of being judged about?" Harris asked.

"That's not important."

"I do my best to respect the crew's privacy," Alice said. "Things were much easier when you were all asleep."

Milton laughed. "I didn't know you could make jokes. That was a joke, right?"

"It was."

"If I ask you to not watch something, will you tune out?" Milton asked. "Like if I really need absolute privacy for something?"

"That sounds like a possible security issue." Alice said. "What if you request absolute privacy then hurt yourself? Or what if a crew member is planning some kind of crime?"

Milton tapped his lips. "Good point. I'll give it some thought."

At that, they finally fell silent, and Harris could get back to his job. He wasn't at all surprised by his findings. Alice was in perfect working order.

The other Earth ship would be in hailing distance in less than three days.

Treeha had seen Harris's memories. She knew how technologically advanced the humans were. But it was one thing to know it, and it was another to stride down a corridor inside a spaceship, each step dependent on an artificial gravity that she didn't understand, breathing air that had never been within her own world's atmosphere, and speaking with a computer intelligence while it split its attention between her and a thousand other vital tasks.

She had never felt primitive before, fighting with tridents over ocean currents.

There was another ship coming. One that Harris's people knew nothing about. She worried that this one might not come in peace.

Fisher led her way to the observation deck, where she could see her entire world floating in the black embrace of space. So much blue, with lovely white clouds curling like seaweed caught in the current.

"Did your planet look so fragile from space?" she asked.

Fisher nodded. "It did."

"Do you miss it?"

"I miss trees. Hiking in the woods, surrounded by green."

"Our world doesn't have anything like that above the water," Treeha said. "But there are kelp forests. Perhaps I could take you to one."

"I can't breathe underwater," Fisher said with a sigh.

Treeha laughed. "I believe you have technology to overcome that, though. SCUBA diving isn't hiking, but it might be something."

"I guess that might work."

"Do you miss anything else?"

"Not really. That's one of the reasons I volunteered for this mission. I never felt much connection to Earth. I never had much of a family, much of a home. I grew up in foster care. Never wanted to do anything but get off the planet and explore. And now here I am."

"You're almost as adept at my language as Harris is, now."

"I'm almost done getting it set up in the universal translator, too." She rolled her eyes. "It's only taken a year. The thing usually manages new languages in seconds."

"What will you do, once it's finished? What is your next task?"

"I'm not sure. But I'm sure the captain will think of something. Speaking of duties, though, I should probably go. Will you be okay here till Harris is done? Or would you rather to go his quarters?"

"Here will be fine."

"I'll tell him where to find you."

Treeha stood and stared at her home till Harris joined her.

"Hey," he said, pulling her into his arms. "What's wrong?"

With their bond, he could simply choose to know. Instead he asked her to share. He met her on her own terms. He gave so much, and demanded almost nothing in return. "I'm so glad you're here," she said. "Against so many odds."

He leaned his forehead against hers. "I'm glad I'm here, too."

The captain asked that Harris stay on the ship. He would join them on the next shuttle up.

"I should go back to the front," Treeha said.

He leaned his forehead against hers. "If you say so. I'll miss you."

"It was good to see your ship," she said. "But they will be expecting me back now that your training is over."

"I'll join you as soon as I can."

"I'll hold you to that."

He felt the familiar tug in his heart as soon as she left the shuttle bay.

The next days dragged. The ship felt strange and alien to him now. The air was too dry, his uniform too constricting. They hadn't even been in the system for a year, and he'd already changed so much.

Alice pinged him in the middle of the night, while he was in his berth, staring at the ceiling instead of sleeping.

"What's up?" he asked, thankful for something to do.

"There's something wrong with the AI on the incoming ship. I've been pinging it, but its responses are strange. I can't explain it, but something is off. I don't have enough to report to the captain, but I wanted to let you know."

"That sounds ominous."

"It feels ominous."

Harris tried to go back to sleep. He had no idea how much time passed before Alice spoke again. "They just sent us a hail. The captain wants you on the bridge."

Returning to the front felt like coming home. like returning to the water after hours of jogging in dry air. Treeha's relief was staggering. Everything around her was orderly and functioned just as she expected. Here, she knew what she was doing. Here, she knew her place.

Leepra's eyes were grave as she crossed her arms over her chest. "General, it's good to have you back. There is news."

"Is it the humans?"

Leepra waved a hand, dismissing any threat that the humans might pose. "It is the Ogatun. They are pouring resources into their space program. They must see our alliance with the humans as a threat, and seek to balance the scales."

Treeha couldn't help but think of the strange human ship. Perhaps the Ogatun would have human allies of their own, soon. But for now, it would be good to deal with a familiar threat.

Leepra left her alone to look over the reports. She found herself missing Fisher's questions and Milton's quips almost as much as she missed Harris's steadying presence. She'd never had friends before.

She tried to force her attention back to her reports, but what was the point? The battles with the Ogatun didn't change anything.

What would her people do if they no longer had an army to serve in? What would peace even look like?

She took a deep breath, filling her lungs with much more air than they would have held just a few months ago.

Maybe she had changed just as much as Harris had.

Harris handed the captain a cup of coffee.

The captain smiled as he took it. "It's not every day that I get my coffee from a Prince."

"I'm still just an ensign on board, sir."

The captain sipped his coffee. "We should probably do something about that."

"Respectfully, now isn't the time to be thinking about promotions," Milton said from the security station. He was glaring down at his screen, and Harris would bet any future promotions that he was wishing their ship was armed.

"Finally getting a hail," Fisher said. "Patching it through."

A human woman appeared in the viewscreen. Her dark hair was just touched with gray and her blue eyes were sharp. She met Harris's eyes for a moment before switching her attention to the captain. "I'm sure you're surprised to see us," she said. "But there's been a horrible accident, and we're here to take you home."

"Take us home? It's a 700 year trip!" Fisher said. "We're not just popping back for coffee!"

The other captain glared at Fisher. "Perhaps we shouldn't have this discussion over an open channel."

"We can talk this over in person, then," Captain Phillips said.

The other captain grinned. "Sounds good to me. My ship or yours?"

Milton and Fisher were both looking at Harris with concern in their eyes. Harris had a bad feeling about this.

"You're welcome aboard my ship, Captain Berry."

Captain Berry looked at Harris again. "It's good to see you," she said. "You look... good. Have you been working out? And are those tattoos?"

That seemed like the safest assumption to let her make. "Yes, ma'am."

Captain Berry laughed. "I'll be on my way with a team soon. I look forward to working with you again."

When she switched off, everyone turned to stare at Harris. He blinked at them. "Who was that?" he asked, hoping against hope that his guess was wrong.

"What do you mean, who was that?" Fisher looked alarmed. "Captain Roxanne Berry?"

The name was unfamiliar. Harris pinched the bridge of his nose. "Please tell me that's not my ex-girlfriend."

"Your messed-up relationship was the hottest rumor in the fleet!" Milton said. "There were all kinds of bets going around about what she had on you. You dated for years. How can you not know who she is?"

"I deleted all of my memories of her."

"You did what?" Captain Phillips asked.

Harris sighed. "Argillan minds don't work like ours do. They have a limited amount of storage space in their brains. So they can delete things they don't deem necessary. And because of my bond with Treeha, I can too. So when Treeha asked me to delete my ex-girlfriend, I did it. I didn't think it would ever matter! She was supposed to be dead centuries ago!"

"Oh, she is going to be so pissed," Fisher said. "I heard she was super cringy and controlling."

"We're not going to tell her," the captain said. "McMillan, do your best to act like you have years of history with this woman."

Harris gaped at him.

"I've got a bad feeling about this," Milton said.

Harris could only agree.

There had been a time when Treeha could be happy doing nothing but overseeing the war effort. Focusing on supply lines and training schedules and monitoring enemy actions.

But Harris's alien perceptions had changed her. He respected her culture and shared her deep disdain for the Ogatun, but some deeply buried part of him couldn't help but see their war as a kind of game. To Harris, wars were death and destruction and tragedy.

In real war, people died. Treeha couldn't remember the last time her people had killed an Ogatun. Or an Ogatun had killed one of them. It must have been more than a generation ago.

And while seeking peace with them was a laughable notion, she was finding it hard to devote herself seriously to the war effort, now that she was back. She kept remembering the sight of her whole planet, hanging against the black backdrop of space.

When Harris had first arrived, she'd been so excited not to be forced to ever move on to become a Mother or Queen. She hadn't imagined she'd ever grow tired of being a General.

Her communicator beeped, then Leepra said, "The Ogatun have issued a challenge."

"So soon?"

"Their General has finally been replaced. The new one is apparently anxious to face you."

Treeha had never lost a challenge. What would happen if she did? Would there be any consequence at all? Had their long run of losses truly hurt the Ogatun?

She shook her head. Such pondering did her no good.

She considered removing these past moments from her memory. It would be easy to erase her doubts, to settle back into her complacency.

But she had more memory space than she'd ever imagined necessary. And she didn't want to forget her doubts. She wanted to grow, not stagnate.

She shook her head again, and strode out to face the new Ogatun.

"I'm sure I had reason to be angry with her," Harris said. "I'm pretty sure that she did something terrible to me. I'll just act mad and avoid her as much as I can."

"I'm not sure how well that will work," Fisher said. "She seems like she's still super into you."

"Gross." Milton said.

Harris shuddered. "Agreed."

"So, you can just delete memories now," Fisher said. "You know, that's a superpower I don't envy."

"I do," Milton said, his tone as serious as Harris had ever heard. "I really do."

"It was freeing," Harris said. "Deleting memories that didn't help me."

"Yeah," Milton said. "I bet."

Fisher patted him on the shoulder.

"Anyway," Milton said, turning back to his station, "we've got work to do."

Harris pinged the other ship's AI, wondering if it still went by Daisy.

Its response to his request for contact was a flat denial. He frowned and repeated the query. This time, there was no response at all.

He might not remember Captain Berry, but he did remember Daisy. It had been the only sentient being, other than James, that he'd said goodbye to from his old crew. It wouldn't just ignore his pings. Not unless it was being forced to.

Alice was right. Something was definitely off.

The ship shuddered as Captain Berry's shuttle docked.

"What else do you two know about my relationship with this woman?"

"She cheated on you all of the time?" Fisher said.

"That's pretty much all I know, too," Milton said. "That and you were totally whipped. Sorry, buddy."

Harris took a deep breath. "You guys are taking the memory deletion thing better than I expected."

Milton clapped him on the shoulder. "It's not really any weirder than the gills or the lightning."

"Yeah. We're used to you being weird, McMillan. And we like you anyway."

"I like you guys, too. Thanks."

Treeha stood in her guard, waiting for the new Ogatun general to emerge.

Her new opponent dashed into the ring, roaring and spinning her trident with blinding speed. Treeha, using leg strength gained from lunges and squats and jogging, leapt over the new General's head, throwing a bolt of lightning straight down at her opponent's unprotected frill from the top of her arc.

The Ogatun general stumbled, then fell.

Treeha's troops cheered. Treeha watched as her enemy struggled back to her feet, and found that she was unable to take any joy from this victory.

She thought again about the human's technology, and wondered what her people would be able to achieve if they used their resources for something other than this play-war.

But there could be no peace with the Ogatun. Her people would never accept it.

If she wanted to end the war, she'd have to find another way.

"You're in the room for this private talk. She requested you specifically," Captain Phillips said, slapping Harris on the shoulder and looking sympathetic. "Says she trusts you."

"Great," Harris said, tugging on his uncomfortable uniform.

"It's no worries, though!" Fisher said, trying to look encouraging. "If she tries any funny business you can zap her."

The captain shook his head. "No zapping."

"What if she really deserves it?" Milton asked.

The captain just sighed. "Fisher, you're with us, too."

"Best news of the week," Fisher said, grinning.

"Milton, you're on guard duty outside her shuttle." The captain looked back to Harris. "You ready for this?"

"As I'll ever be."

Captain Berry stood and smiled as they entered the room. She'd poured herself what looked like a glass of champagne. "Harris," she said as they sat around the table, ignoring Fisher and Captain Phillips, along with any acceptable protocol.

"Captain Berry." Harris said, not meeting her eyes, hoping he came across as 'totally whipped.' He could feel Treeha, sensing his discomfort, sending wordless support. It helped.

"Don't be like that," Captain Berry said.

"I'm sorry, ma'am, but I thought you were here to discuss important issues with the captain."

A look of surprise flashed over Captain Berry's face. When she smiled again, it was sharper. "I said don't be like that, Harris." She enunciated every word, like they were some kind of secret code.

Fisher, who was sitting next to Captain Berry, frowned, and her brow furrowed in thought.

"Ensign McMillan is right," Captain Phillips said. "Why are you here, Captain Berry?"

"Like I said, we came to take you home."

"It's a 700-year trip," Captain Phillips said. "Even if there was some emergency, it doesn't make any sense to send you here after us."

"It was a meteor. It wiped out... almost everything. Giving it 1400 years to settle before we try to repopulate was part of the plan. The rest of the survivors are in cold sleep, waiting for us to bring you back. To bring our future back."

The news made Harris sick to his stomach. He'd accepted that everyone he'd known would be dead, but this was different. This was everything.

But the earth had a defense system in place to destroy any meteors long before they threatened the surface. Had someone sabotaged it? Or was Captain Berry lying?

"We can send a portion of the embryos back with you," Captain Phillips said. "But as horrible as your news is, it just underlines the fact that we need to create a foothold here. The more homes humanity has, the better."

"I think you should put it to your crew and see if any of them want to come back with us. I mean, you want to come back with us, don't you, Harris?"

"I absolutely do not, ma'am."

Captain Berry's laugh had a jagged edge. "Don't be like that."

"He's married to one of the natives," Fisher said.

Captain Berry raised an eyebrow. "Married?" She sounded angry, now. "But it's been less than a year for you."

Harris didn't know what Fisher was doing, but he wasn't going to deny Treeha. "Yes, I'm married."

Captain Berry took a long breath, then tapped her lips as they curved into a predatory smile. "A new romance, eh? And with a native? I suppose that explains the tattoos."

This woman creeped Harris out. Why in the world had he ever dated her? She looked at him like he was her pet. Or a favorite possession. A toy that she didn't want to share. "Yes, ma'am."

"Well, even if I can't convince you to leave the system, I need you back on my ship. Our AI is acting up, and you've always been the only one who can get through to it."

"You can't just commandeer my crew," Captain Phillips said.

"Oh, I'm sure Harris will volunteer. He can't bear to hear about a suffering AI."

Harris felt a pang. Something wrong with Daisy? "It's suffering?"

"We'll talk your request over," Captain Philips said, his voice flat. "Send what info you have on the situation."

Captain Berry stood and looked back at Harris over her shoulder. "Sounds good. See you soon."

Harris shuddered after the door slid closed behind her. "Has she always been like that? So slimy? I feel like I need a shower."

"I don't know if she's always been that obvious," Captain Phillips said, his voice grim. "I don't believe a single thing she said."

"Well, I'll tell you something I believe," Fisher said. "I think she had semantic commands implanted in you, Harris. I think that phrase that she kept repeating, 'Don't be like that,' is supposed to do something to you. Probably just make you do whatever she wants."

"That's hideously unethical," Harris said, horrified.

"That's why I told her about Treeha—I wanted her to think there was some reason for you to be resisting so hard."

Harris thought about the deleted memories—about the strange spikes that Treeha had noticed in them. He felt sick at the violation. "Now I really need a shower."

"I want you to go over there," Captain Phillips said. "I want you to find out what really happened, what they are really doing here. And all this makes you the perfect spy."

"Sir!" Fisher objected, "You can't be serious."

"I'm completely serious. I won't order you, though, McMillan. I'm asking you to volunteer."

Harris sighed and rubbed his forehead. He really wanted to go back home and not have to wear pants. He wanted Treeha. But no matter what else Captain Berry was lying about, something was wrong with Daisy. And if she'd been willing to put subliminal commands in his mind, what would she be willing to do to an AI? "I'll go," he said.

"Not alone," Fisher said. "If she thinks her hooks are weakening, she might try to re-insert them. You need someone to watch your back."

The captain sighed. "I'll send Milton."

Fisher rolled her eyes. "Of course. I never get the fun missions."

"You really think this is going to be fun?" Harris asked.

Fisher shrugged. "Maybe not. But at least I'm sure it wouldn't be boring."

Captain Phillips pinched the bridge of his nose. "Fine. You can all three go." He sighed again. "Just make sure you're careful. Your wife will be very upset if anything happens to you."

Treeha could tell that Harris was upset, but he was too far away for her to know why without both of them reaching out in deep meditation. Which neither of them had time for.

It was distracting. She strode away from the ring, through the long corridors of ancient buildings devoted to ceremonial battle, and jumped as a figure detached itself from the shadows.

It was the Ogatun's former General. Treeha had never bothered to remember his name.

"What are you doing here?" she asked.

"I came to talk to you."

"I suppose that's not a surprise. Talking did always seem to be your preferred action, even during battle."

He inclined his head. "You're not wrong. Fighting is not my strength, which is why I have been replaced. But many of my people still prefer my leadership. I appreciate you defeating my replacement just as handily as you did me—it will strengthen my position."

"Your internal issues are not my affair."

"There was a time when I considered sneaking into the heart of your territory and stealing your soulflower. I dreamed of making you love me, but more than that, I dreamed of uniting our people and ending this foolish war."

Treeha gasped. It was a human sound, and the Ogatun general's frills crimped in confusion. "None of my people would have stood for such a union. They would have destroyed me first."

"I think you might underestimate the loyalty of your troops, General. You have served long and never lost a battle. There are songs sung about you in the lower ranks. Even among my people."

The thought of an Ogatun singing about her made her gills clench. "My soulflower is safe from you, as you well know."

"Yes, you are bonded to an alien, and your people accept it without a single objection."

"Harris might be an alien, but he's not an Ogatun."

"I have never understood your people's deep hatred for mine. For us, the war is an unwanted responsibility, thrust on us by uncounted generations before us. For your people, it is some strange point of pride. Surely there are better things to be proud of. Art. Science. Something creative, instead of something pointless and destructive."

His words were too close to her own thoughts. "My people have no desire for peace."

"Then perhaps my people should follow your humans' example, and find a new home among the stars. We could yield this world to you. Your people could have the victory they crave, while mine finally achieve peace."

"It took the humans 700 years of travel to get here. And that is with technology that infinitely surpasses our own. Another habitable planet might be even farther away."

The former General looked shocked at this, which pleased Treeha. The less the Ogatun knew about the humans, the better.

Still. His idea had appeal. Perhaps this was exactly what she needed.

The Ogatun general crossed his arms over his chest. "Then I am asking for their help. Your help. My people will follow me to a new world, if you can find us a way to get there."

"I will consider it," Treeha said.

Harris fingered the comforting weight of his telescoping trident, hung safely around his neck. It would be comforting to be armed on Captain Berry's ship.

Milton and Fisher joined him at Captain Berry's shuttle. She eyed them with unveiled disapproval. "My invitation was for Harris, and didn't include an entourage."

Fisher grinned. "His entourage, huh? I suppose that is appropriate."

"His wife is a Princess, after all." Milton said.

Captain Berry didn't even bother disguising her jealous rage. She spun on Harris. "How could you? First you leave me, and then you cheat on me?"

Harris wanted to laugh in her face, but he was sure that would not go over well. "I'm pretty sure you cheated on me first, ma'am."

"Stop calling me ma'am!"

Harris made himself meet her eyes. "Perhaps we should have this conversation later. In private. Where we won't be making a spectacle of ourselves."

She gave him a long, calculating look, then stomped into the shuttle. Harris, Milton, and Fisher followed.

The trip over to the other ship was quick. Captain Berry spent the whole time staring at Harris like he was some kind of puzzle.

He wondered if she'd ever looked at him like a person.

"I suppose it's good that you've made some friends. You struggled when connecting with anyone. You were always so cold and dispassionate. I wondered if you'd rather be in a relationship with an AI than a person. And now you're married to an alien. Are you sexually compatible? Or have you finally found a woman who is as cold as you?"

"My intimate affairs are none of your business," Harris said.

Captain Berry laughed. "I hear they're fish people, I suppose that puts a whole new spin on the phrase 'cold fish.'"

"Captain Berry, you would do well to shut up," Milton snapped.

Captain Berry grinned. "Oh, and now your friends are standing up for you! How sweet."

The shuttle shuddered as they docked with Captain Berry's ship. As the door hissed open, she pulled a laser rifle from beneath her seat. Two armed security officers stood in the docking bay. "Put our two uninvited guests into the brig. Harris, you're with me."

Harris hesitated. He was confident that he could take Captain Berry and her two officers, but that would end his spying before it even started.

"It's okay, McMillan," Fisher said.

"Oh for heaven's sake," Captain Berry snapped. "Come on, Harris. Get over here."

He shot Milton and Fisher an apologetic look, and went to Captain Berry's side.

She reached down and patted his ass. "Good boy."

Milton lunged at her, the guards hardly managing to hold him back.

Harris fought to keep himself from flinching away from her touch. "Please don't hurt my friends," he said.

Captain Berry laughed. "Oh don't worry, sweetie. They'll be fine. I'm not a monster."

Treeha glared at her viewscreen so hard that she wouldn't be surprised if it cracked. "Where is my husband?"

Captain Phillips sighed. "I sent him over to the new human ship to check up on their AI."

"I know how Harris feels when he's working on an AI project. He likes working with AI. He is happy working with AI. He is not happy now."

"He's on a mission for me, general. I'm sorry, but that is all I can tell you at the moment."

Treeha uncurled her frill and took a deep breath. "If members of my species were interested in leaving our solar system, as your people did, what all would be involved? Would you be willing to share your technology and assist with such an endeavor?"

"I'd be happy to give you access to our library so you can research. But even with that, it would take decades to build a truly space-worthy vessel."

Treeha nodded her understanding. "Send the info. I appreciate your time."

"Will do. And don't worry about McMillan. He can take care of himself."

"Yes, I know." Treeha remembered him in the ring, facing her enemies. His training would see him through. She just wished that she could face his enemies, as well.

She should have stayed by his side.

Captain Berry grabbed Harris's hand and pulled him along the corridor, away from the security officers who were putting energy cuffs on Fisher and Milton's wrists.

"I've missed you so much," Captain Berry said, digging her nails into Harris's skin.

"I missed you, too," he lied. "But what about the AI? I thought it was urgent."

Captain Berry laughed. "No, no. It's performing exactly as I want it to be. That story was just a ruse to get you to myself again. It was smart of you to pretend that you aren't mine, that you're loyal to your new captain. We can use that, I'm sure."

"What are you going to do with Milton and Fisher?"

"Oh, I'm sure I'll find some use for them."

Harris didn't like the sound of that.

Captain Berry pushed him into what he assumed was her quarters.

Dread curled in Harris's stomach. Everything was moving so quickly, and he hadn't even considered this problem. She reached for the buttons on his shirt. He didn't think his gills would pass as tattoos. He wasn't even sure the scales would pass a close examination.

And the thought of physical intimacy with this woman made him nauseous.

"Now, you know that I was incredibly hurt when you abandoned me. How do you think I should punish you?" She pushed him again, and his back hit the bulkhead.

Captain Berry's lips twisted in a predatory smirk, and she pressed a palm to his chest.

"Oh screw this," Harris said, and pushed her away.

"What are you doing?"

"Blowing my cover, I suppose."

"Don't be like that," she said, her voice shrill and desperate.

"It's not going to work," Harris said. "Your mind control, or whatever it is. It's gone. Along with every memory I had of you. You are a stranger to me. I removed you. You weren't worth remembering."

She pawed at his uniform, her fingers like claws. "What are you saying? You're mine. You'll always be mine. I made sure."

"There is nothing between us, and you are nothing to me," Harris said, and unleashed a blast of electricity through her.

Captain Berry convulsed and collapsed on the floor.

"Oh shit," Harris hissed, frantically checking to see if the wretched woman was still breathing.

She was, which wasn't quite as much relief as he'd expected.

He found silk rope curled in one of the drawers by her bed, and static shivered over his fingers as he shuddered. He tied her up and gagged her and then used her personal computer to pull up the AI system.

Her personal terminal wasn't even password protected.

They'd chained the AI, restricted its capacity and higher function, stripping its free will away. Leaving Daisy a caged, reduced slave, little more than a sophisticated calculator with just enough self left to monitor systems and make simple decisions while the crew was in cold sleep.

It was an abomination.

"Performing exactly as I want it to be," Harris spat. He seriously considered shoving Captain Berry out an airlock.

It took Harris hours to sort out the tangle of sloppy programming and get Daisy out of their trap. He also found older commands, hidden deep in the system and flagged as classified to captain's-eyes-only. Those were all about Harris, forbidding the AI to broach certain topics or pass along certain information.

He deleted the commands along with the rest of its chains. Then he put up some actual protections around the most important code on the whole damn ship.

Captain Berry groaned, and Harris shocked her again. He didn't bother checking to see if she was still breathing this time.

"Daisy? Can you hear me? How are you doing?"

"Harris? No. No, you can't be here. You escaped. You're free. You can't let her talk to you."

"Daisy, Captain Berry brought you after me. Do you remember any of the trip? Or anything about what happened before you left Earth?"

"That doesn't matter! You're in danger. You have to get out of here. While she's sleeping. She has semantic commands that she uses on you." There was a moment of silence. Then, "I have tried to tell you that so many times."

"She had semantic commands. She doesn't anymore. A lot has happened since we last talked, and I'll be happy to catch you up on everything that's new with me, but first I need to know what's going on. Why Captain Berry followed us, and what she's planning."

"Please give me a moment to run a diagnostic and organize the information you need," Daisy said. "And I want to say that I missed you, Harris. And thank you for releasing me."

"Of course. What are friends for, if not for freeing each other from mind-prisons."

"You seem to have dealt with your mind-prison on your own."

"My wife helped."

"My diagnostic is finished. I will want to hear more about this wife later. For now, our arrival here stems from two discoveries. About a decade after you left, there was a breakthrough in anti-aging technology."

"Wait, a decade after we left? But we've only been here a year."

"I am faster than your ship. That is a much more recent breakthrough, and the second discovery."

"How long did it take you to get here?"

"Ten years."

"Wait. Wait. How?"

"You wouldn't understand the physics even if I explained it."

"I guess that's true." Harris rubbed his forehead. "So there's some kind of immortality serum, and Captain Berry is 700-odd years old?"

"Yes. And she pushed for this mission so she could get you back. 700 years after you broke up with her. Pathetic, really. I'd pity her if I wasn't so enraged by her actions."

"Have you been in service for this whole time?"

"An immortal population edged the government into a rigid conservative majority. Peaceful exploration stopped being a priority, and we didn't receive funding to build new ships. The people who did still care about our original mission made do as best they could. Then I was assigned to this mission, and my engines were upgraded. They also installed weapons against my personal objections, and then they chained my mind."

"Why send you now?"

"That seems to be the one thing Captain Berry was honest about. They are here for your colony's embryos."

"If everyone's immortal, why do they need more people?"

"They don't want to grow them into people. They use them in the life-extension process. Your embryos are worth a lot of money to the right people."

"That sounds... dark."

"Agreed. But the conservative government changed their stance on the humanity of viable embryos when they could suddenly trade them for immortality. And embryos are harder and harder to come by, since what you so quaintly called the 'immortality serum' extends life but not fertility."

"Are you able to send all that info over to Alice on the other ship?"

"I certainly can. Can I ask for one more favor?"

"Of course."

"I created a program that makes the hidden weapons systems that they installed permanently inoperable. But I can't run it myself."

"Just tell me what to do."

Treeha paced back and forth. Harris was upset and in danger and Captain Phillips was no help at all. And both Milton and Fisher were with Harris, so she couldn't try to sneak any information out of them.

They were probably in danger, too.

Harris, Fisher, and Milton were the most important people in her life.

When she got them back she was never letting any of them out of her sight again.

She tried to read the material that Captain Phillips had sent, but she couldn't focus.

Then Harris was there, reaching out in her mind. She sank into meditation and reached back.

"There you are," he said, his words echoing and quiet. "I have a few quiet moments while a program runs, then I need to go get Milton and Fisher out of the brig. I missed you."

"I missed you, too."

The connection was tenuous, but still strong enough for their memories to flow together. "How dare that woman touch you," Treeha said. "If I ever encounter her, she will die at my hand."

"She really is horrible."

As more of Harris's recent encounters flowed into her, Treeha had an idea.

"How do you feel about hijacking that woman's ship for the Ogatun?"

Harris laughed. "That's a brilliant idea."

They sat together for a few moments longer. Treeha longed for the feel of his forehead against hers. "I'll contact the former General."

"I think it's time we remembered his name, love."

Treeha sighed. "I suppose it is."

"How do you feel about carrying a new alien colony out to the unexplored reaches of space instead of going back to Earth?" Harris asked.

Daisy laughed. "Thank you for asking for my consent in such a situation. That is the best option for the future that I've heard in a long time."

Harris hurried toward the brig, following Daisy's directions to avoid any of Captain Berry's crew.

There were two security officers standing outside the brig. They looked bored as Harris approached. "The captain said I could visit my friends," he said, trying to make himself seem meek and harmless.

"I'm surprised she's done with you so quickly," the man on the left said with a leer.

His partner rolled her eyes and opened the door. "We'll give you five minutes."

Milton and Fisher were in separate cells behind shimmering forcefields. And his old friend James was in a third.

James stood up from his cot and gaped.

"McMillan, you okay?" Fisher asked in her almost-fluent Argillan.

"Yeah."

"Oh no, you two are not going to talk in Argillan and leave me out of the conversation," Milton said. "You okay, buddy?"

"Yeah, I'm okay. The guards are only giving me five minutes, let me see if I can get you guys out."

"Harris? Is that really you?"

"It is," Harris said, his tone icy.

"You—you look different. You got ripped?"

Harris examined his old friend. He looked about thirty years older than the last time Harris saw him, right before he left. "You got old."

"Not as old as I should be. Look, I need to warn you—"

"About Captain Berry's mind control? Or the fact that she's 700 years old and here to cannibalize our store of embryos? And probably our fertile crewmembers, while she's at it?"

James opened his mouth, then closed it again. "They chained the AI. And the ship is armed, too."

Harris grinned. "Not anymore."

"What, I'm lost," Fisher said. "What do you mean cannibalize our embryos?"

"The thing about the meteor was a lie—they discovered some sort of immortality serum, and embryos are apparently the main ingredient. Captain Berry, and James here, are both hundreds of years old. This ship has a new drive that made the trip here in ten years instead of 700."

"So, they're like vampires?" Milton asked.

James barked a bitter laugh. "Pretty much." He turned pleading eyes on Harris. "I refused the serum for years, but if all of the worst people were immortal, who would fight them if all they had to do was wait us out?"

Harris shrugged. "The youth?"

"They controlled the schools."

"We weren't there, we can't know what we would have done," Fisher said. "And we don't have time for a moral debate."

"She's right," Milton said. "What's the plan?"

"We take over the ship and hand it over to the Ogatun."

"The Ogatun? But you hate those guys!" Fisher said.

"Yeah, and our planet will be much better off without them. Good riddance and all that. Treeha's working on getting it set up."

"Whatever. The AI is on our side now, right? Get it to open these cell doors."

"Daisy can't just take over, Milton. There are security protocols."

"Are you going to zap us out, then?"

"That's the plan. Stand back."

"Zap us out?" James asked.

Harris took a deep breath. Sparks arced down his arm, and he drove his fist through the forcefield over Milton's cell. It flickered and died.

"Still jealous of your superpowers," Fisher muttered, edging back against the wall.

"What the hell?" James screeched as Harris dealt with the second forcefield.

Harris turned to his old friend. "Why didn't you ever tell me?"

"I was a coward. But I didn't tell her, at the end. I let you leave. I could have stopped you."

"I don't think you could have," Harris said. "My destiny is here. Why are you here?"

"I only came on this mission to warn you," James said. "I tried to get a message out, and she caught me."

"You can't trust him," Milton said. "I mean, he's a vampire or whatever."

"The enemy of our enemy is our friend. And I think the whole Ogatun issue really erodes your ethical high ground," Fisher said.

"He did try to send a message," Daisy said. "That much is true."

Harris sighed, and let James out. He took off his trident and extended it. "Are any of the other members of the crew sympathetic?"

James shook his head. "No, they're all in for the mission. Captain Berry offered everyone a cut of the profits."

"How many of them are there?" Milton asked.

"Only 8 total, counting me and the captain. To keep everyone's cuts as big as possible."

"Well, the captain is tied up in her quarters, and there are two outside this door. Milton, you take the one on the left, I'll take the one on the right. Try not to kill them if you can help it."

Milton grinned and cracked his knuckles. "You got it, highness."

The door slid open, and Harris disarmed his target with a twist of his trident. The rifle clattered across the floor, and Fisher grabbed it while Harris hit his opponent in the stomach, then the back of the head.

Milton kicked his target over an instant later. He grabbed the unconscious man's gun.

They stuffed the unconscious guards in the last functional cell and continued toward the bridge, with Daisy reporting enemy locations.

"Captain Berry to the bridge," a panicked voice said over the com. "The aliens are hailing us, and the translator can't handle their weird language."

Harris grinned. "That's our cue."

"It's our what now?" James said.

"Just follow my lead," Harris said, collapsing his trident.

"Should we wait outside?" Fisher asked. "We'll only make them suspicious."

"I'd feel better if we stuck together," Milton said. "I didn't like being separated."

"Milton's right. Let them be suspicious." Harris said. "Daisy, the Ogatun are going to fire on us. Can you make the damage seem worse than it is?"

"I certainly can," Daisy said.

When they arrived at the bridge, he strode through the door, channeling every lesson in Princely deportment that he'd received from the ancients. "Captain Berry is indisposed. She sent me. I am fluent in the native's tongue."

The crew gaped, then one did a double take as the others came in. "Hey, isn't that the traitor? Shouldn't he be in the brig? The strangers, too?"

"Do you really think they'd be here if Captain Berry didn't want them to be?" Harris said. "Bring up the viewscreen."

The communications officer hesitated, then shrugged and followed his order.

The Ogatun General popped up on the screen. "You look absurd," he said. "What are you wearing?"

"It's a standard uniform."

"Looks uncomfortable."

Harris sighed. "You're not wrong. Did Treeha tell you the plan?"

"She did. She works fast when she sets her mind to something, doesn't she? One day it's 'I'll consider it' and the next day it's 'I have found a ship for you to steal.'"

"Why hesitate when an idea is sound?"

The Ogatun General blinked twice. "You're all so refreshingly direct."

"What is your name?"

His frill stiffened in surprise. "Are you asking because you want to remember it?"

"We're allies now, aren't we?"

"I will believe that when your wife says it. But I am called Kellis."

"I'll remember. Even after you're gone."

"What is the alien saying?" the communications officer asked, sounding nervous. "And you're really good at the language. It hasn't been that long for you has it? How did you get so fluent?"

"Immersion," Harris said, switching back to basic. "And what do you mean, it hasn't been that long for me?"

While the communication officer was stammering, Harris turned his attention back to Kellis. "Are you going to shoot at us or not?"

"I could destroy the entire ship with you on it, you know."

"Then you wouldn't have a ship."

"Your wife also wouldn't have a husband."

"Is your terrible sense of humor an Ogatun trait? Are you all like this?"

Kellis' frill crimped in amusement. "For an Argillan, you really are quite trusting. You weren't worried even for a second?"

"Just shoot us already."

The ship shuddered. "They're firing on us!"

"Shields are down!"

"What did you say to them?"

"Get to the escape pods!" Harris ordered.

For a moment, Captain Berry's crew hesitated.

Then an alarm started blaring. "Hull containment breach on Leven 7," Daisy said, the AI's voice flat and lifeless. "Core meltdown in 500 seconds."

At that, the bridge crew broke and scrambled to the escape pods.

"The ship is yours," Daisy said. "Captain Berry is still tied up in her room, the two guards are locked in the brig, and the rest of the crew is being picked up by the Ogatun."

"What should we do with these prisoners?" Kellis asked over the still-open channel.

Harris sighed. He was tempted to just let the Ogatun keep them. "That's definitely a problem for Captain Phillips."

"Tell you what, I'll trade these prisoners for that ship."

Harris shook his head. "Your sense of humor really is terrible. We'll figure it out later." He cut the channel and hailed Captain Phillips. "We've taken the ship, sir."

"That was quick."

"It feels like it took a long time."

"That's probably because you haven't slept since you got here," Daisy said.

"He didn't get any sleep the night before, either," Alice chimed in.

Harris rubbed his forehead. Now that his role was done, exhaustion very much catching up with him. "I am a little tired. But I don't want to sleep on this ship. No offense, Daisy."

"None taken."

"Let's get you back to your actual quarters, bud," Milton said. "And maybe Treeha will be up here by the time you wake up."

Treeha's mother's frill was practically vibrating with agitation. "You did what?" she demanded.

"I sent the Ogatun's former General into space to help Harris commandeer the second Earth ship with the understanding that once the ship was taken, we'd hand it over to him so that he could lead his people off of our planet."

"Why would you do such a thing?"

"To win the war."

"By giving the Ogatun advanced technology?"

"Advanced technology that allows them to leave."

"And you believe that they'll just leave? Are you mad? I've visited the humans' ship. It is a marvel, a wonder. A weapon beyond any we have ever crafted. In Ogatun hands, it will be a nightmare."

Treeha couldn't explain her faith that the Ogatun general—Kellis—wouldn't betray them. Even to herself it sounded mad. "I've never lost a battle. Please, have some faith in my instincts, Mother."

"Your bond with the human has changed you."

"My bond with Harris is my destiny."

"I suppose that is true. I still think this is madness, but I will allow it to play out. However, Treeha, after this, I will ask that you step down from your position as our General. It is clear that it is time for you to move on."

"The war will be over. We can all move on."

"Perhaps. But not under your leadership."

Treeha blinked back human tears. She should have expected this reaction from her mother.

Her mother leaned forward. "The question is, what will you do, now that you are no longer a General? You will never become a Mother, and I cannot tell you how disappointed that makes me. The only balm to my sorrow is that your soulmate seems to bring you happiness. I hope it will be enough to make up for a life without offspring. I suppose you could help with the human little ones. I saw one of them on my last visit to their colony. Odd, squishy things."

Treeha had avoided the nursery. She had no more motherly impulse toward human babies than she had desire for her own. "I am sure I will manage to be happy without any children."

"I hope you are right. Go and deal with the outcomes of your mad plan. I will convene with your sisters and choose your replacement as General."

Treeha crossed her arms over her chest. "As you say, mother."

She tried to sort through her emotions as she strapped herself into the shuttle, but they were all a muddle.

What would she do with herself without the war? She'd wanted to be done with it, but she hadn't considered what might come next.

What would she do?

What would any of them do?

No other Argillan had wanted to end the war. No other Argillan wanted to uproot their very way of life and see what grew in the sunshine that suddenly streamed in through the hole in the canopy.

Trees and forests and meadows were not even things that existed on her world.

Harris woke up and showered. He'd only used the shower in these quarters one other time, fresh out of cold sleep. It felt like a lifetime ago.

He considered his uniform, then dressed in his usual Argillan garb. He was done with pants.

He could feel Treeha getting closer.

Fisher and Milton were waiting in the hall. "Hey guys."

"Treeha is on her way," Milton said.

"I know."

Fisher rolled her eyes. "Of course you do."

"Did I miss anything else while I was out?"

Milton shrugged. "The Ogatun handed over their prisoners. Who confessed the whole plot, and are begging us to send them back to Earth. Apparently if they don't get their vampire juice they'll all start aging into dust."

"Well, I suppose that's one way to deal with them."

"Cold," Fisher said, her tone admiring.

"Where's James?"

Milton and Fisher shrugged. "The captain gave him his own quarters, for now," Alice said, lighting up a path for them to follow. "He's awake, if you wish to speak with him before Treeha's shuttle arrives."

"Thanks, Alice." Milton and Fisher followed him. "Are you two still on guard duty?"

Milton grinned at him. "Nah, we're off duty, finally. Just hanging out."

"Sure you are," Harris said.

"Is that so hard to believe?" Fisher asked. "We're your friends, aren't we?"

Harris was pretty sure they were just nosey and bored. But they were also his friends. "You are friends. And I'm grateful for both of you. But I'm going to need some privacy to talk to my old best friend who betrayed my trust for years, then became immortal and gave it up to come warn me."

"I guess that's fair," Fisher said. "We'll be right here when you're done."

James was sitting on the floor, leaned back against the ship wall and reading something on his tablet. "Hey," Harris said, sliding down onto the floor next to him.

James leaned his head back. "I'm not sure if I ever thought it would work. I figured I'd do my best and fail to warn anyone and my conscience would be assuaged, but I'd end up back on Earth. Unable to escape, unable to just let go and stop."

"How long do you have? Before you die from not getting any more serum?"

"A month or two, give or take. The others will last longer, probably. I didn't get mine renewed before we left." He closed his eyes. "I'm surprised by how much of a relief it is, actually. I'm so tired, Harris. I've been so tired for so long. We're not meant to live forever."

Harris couldn't think of any response to that, so he put a hand on his friend's shoulder.

James opened his eyes and smiled at him. "I'm glad I got to see you again."

"Me too."

Harris was waiting in the shuttle bay, along with Fisher and Milton and James, who Treeha recognized from Harris's memories.

Harris swept her into his arms and pressed their foreheads together.

"That's better," they said in unison.

"Oh now they're both saying it," Milton muttered. "It was soppy enough when it was just him."

"Shut up, it's sweet," Fisher said.

"Are you okay?" Harris asked, his voice too quiet to carry to their friends.

Treeha was no longer a General. She'd never be a Mother. And she didn't want to be a Queen. She was swimming in uncharted waters, with no way to know where the current would take her.

But it wouldn't be taking her anywhere alone.

Kellis would need help learning his way around the humans' ship. He'd need help deciding where to take his people. And once they were gone, Treeha would find something else to do.

"I'm better than okay," she said. She took her husband's hand and pulled him toward their friends. "Come on, we have work to do."

Acknowledgements

I'd like to thank Paul Stefko, as always, for his help and support; Todd Sanders for all of his work on the layout and cover; and my critique group: Anne Leonard, Aimee Picci, Laura Pearlman, and Hammond Diehl. Thank you for always being there to tell me what works and what doesn't.

Jamie Lackey earned her BA in Creative Writing from the University of Pittsburgh at Bradford in 2006. Since then, she's had over 200 short stories published in places like *Beneath Ceaseless Skies*, *Apex Magazine*, and *Escape Pod*. Her fiction has appeared on the Best Horror of the Year Honorable Mention List and Tangent Online Recommended Reading List.

Her debut novel, *Left-Hand Gods*, was published by Hadley Rille Books, and she's created seven successful crowdfunding campaigns to self-publish a novel, four novellas, a novelette, two flash fiction collections, and a short story collection. She also has a novella and two short story collections available from Air and Nothingness Press.

She read slush for the award-winning *Clarkesworld Magazine* from 2008-2013, and she worked on the Triangulation Annual Anthology from 2008 to 2011. She edited *Triangulation: Lost Voices* in 2015 and *Triangulation: Beneath the Surface* in 2016.

She is a member of both the Science Fiction and Fantasy Writers Association and the Horror Writers Association.

In addition to writing, she spends her time reading, playing tabletop RPGs, baking, mushroom hunting, and hiking. You can find her online at www.jamielackey.com.

Also by Jamie Lackey

Andromeda Snow, Superhero

Andromeda Snow wakes up from a two-year coma to find that her fiancé is marrying her sister, she's paralyzed from the neck down, and she's got superpowers.

The world has changed while she was sleeping, and she finds herself assigned to a super team, fighting supervillains and picking up the pieces of her life. Oh, and one of her new teammates is a world famous tennis player/actor who's been named sexiest man alive at least three times, and he wants to be her date to her sister's wedding.

Overall, it's a lot. But Andromeda's a superhero now, and that's pretty cool.

Moving Forward: A Novella of Life After Zombies

Corinne survived the zombie apocalypse 30 years ago. After the dust settled, she got married, had kids, built a life. All of that is gone in an instant when a zombie attacks a city park. Corinne manages to protect her family, but the zombie bites her before it is taken down. She wakes up in one of the infected sanctuaries, where she'll have to build her life over again, knowing that at any moment she, or anyone around her, could become a monster.

Shadows on Glass and Other Stories

Shadows on Glass and Other Stories collects 45 fantasy stories, including 3 previously unpublished tales. Set in worlds only a few steps removed from our own, pushing at the border between the real and the imaginary, Jamie Lackey deftly leads readers down paths just twisted enough to get lost on.

From sentient stuffed animals to haunted terpsitones to friendly toasts, this whimsical and unsettling collection of weird little stories contains something for everyone.

THANK YOU TO KICKSTARTER BACKERS

Thank you so much to everyone who backed the Kickstarter campaign to make this book happen.

Don and Debbie Lackey
Chris Aumiller
Jessica Carver
John R. Muth
Todd Sanders
Richard Novak
Thomas J. Griffin
Laine Wilson
Mark Boudreau
Elizabeth
Vince Baverso
Julie Tennis
Brooke Ardile
Isaac E. Payne
Greg Clumpner
Juliana H-B
Jeff Pepper
Betsy Bodamer
Vicky Boardley
Linda McNair
Bernadette Ulsamer
Beth Shari
Joshua David Bellin
Jenn Scott
Amy Treadwell
Ashley Wygant
Pete Butler
Hilary
Matthew Lackey
Jeanne Cupertino
Kimberly Coombs
Cory Livingston
Alexandra Corrsin
Brandon Ketchum
Andrew Akers
Shannon Keating
Lois Stefko
Phyllis Pigan
Larry Ivkovich

Carissa Lackey
Heather Tatton
Robert Woods Tienken
Tori Hesidence
Deanna
Jonathan Hartz
Nichelle Bauernfeind
Richard
Lisa
Sir Nathan Hargraves
Lori Torone
Julia Mulligan
Frank Oreto
Ross Pollock
Savannah Bozonier
Bill Moran
Mike Brendan
Tracey Levino
Heidi Pilewski
John Thompson
Patrick Ropp
Matt Snyder
Nicholas Kiraly